The Hypothetical Girl

The Hypothetical Girl

ELIZABETH COHEN

 Other Press | *New York*

Some of the stories in this collection first appeared in *The Hypothetical Girl and Other Stories of Love in These Times*, published by Split Oak Press, Vestal, New York, in 2011.

Song lyrics on page 91 from "Summertime," from *Porgy and Bess*. Lyrics by DuBose Heyward, music by George Gershwin. Song lyrics on page 91 from "Brother, Can You Spare Me a Dime?" Lyrics by Yip Harburg, music by Jay Gorney.

Production Editor: Yvonne E. Cárdenas
Text Designer: Chris Welch
This book was set in 9.75 pt Iowan by
Alpha Design & Composition of Pittsfield, NH

10 9 8 7 6 5 4 3 2 1

Library of Congress Cataloging-in-Publication Data

Cohen, Elizabeth.
The hypothetical girl / by Elizabeth Cohen.
p. cm.
ISBN 978-1-59051-582-2 (pbk.) — ISBN 978-1-59051-583-9 (ebook)   1. Online dating—Fiction.   2. Dating (Social customs)—Fiction.   3. Domestic fiction.   I. Title.
PS3603.O3465H97 2013
813'.6—dc23
2012036335

Publisher's Note:
This is a work of fiction. Names, characters, places, and incidents either are the product of the author's imagination or are used fictitiously, and any resemblance to actual persons, living or dead, events, or locales is entirely coincidental.

In memory of my mother, Julia,

who might not have approved. (And even if she did, would
· *have said she didn't.)*

Animal Dancing

I t was the time of year when the helicopter seeds twirled down onto the sidewalks like girls showing off at a dance, when the bee balm bushes wore their best purple frocks and the whole world seemed, to Chloe, tricked out for love. Contrary to popular sentiment, Shakespeare and all that, she thought autumn, not spring, was love season. Everything was overripe, lustily clad, luscious beyond luscious, ready to go. She thought of the speech of Proteus from *The Two Gentlemen of Verona*. She had read it in high school and, again, in college:

> *O, how this spring of love resembleth*
> *The uncertain glory of an April day;*
> *Which now shows all the beauty of the sun.*

It should have been an autumn day, not April! It is fall that inspires love. Or maybe spring is the season of love and fall the season of mad lust. Spring for flirting, but fall for the untamed delicious wild thing. Such a line of thinking must have been what did it. Sped her on this frenzied mission, sucked her in on a sudden and surprising rip current of longing.

Each day she tried harder to solve the great search-and-find puzzle of love. She felt just like that; she was looking for men the way you might in one of those word searches, up, down, sideways, backwards, circling all the possibilities. *Could this one be? Could this one . . .*

So far, no go.

Since it was the beginning of the second decade of the new millennium, she was searching, as every modern girl should, on online dating sites, foraging among the pictures and self-described blurbs in the vast fields of the lonely. She had gone on marryme.com, loveforreals .com, and even flirtypants.com, which she thought did not really describe her well but might attract a more exciting sort of man. More the kind she wanted, perhaps. Someone who was ready.

"Fun-loving, nature-adoring, unfancy, smart, and tidy girl," read her profile, after the ninety-seventh edit. It used to say "sex-loving," but that had attracted all kinds of riff-raff, a thoroughly unpleasant herd and even a stalker, so she had toned it down.

"Well hello there," she'd write, night after night, answering the clutter of seekers in her in-box. "Do you like hiking? Sushi? Do you closely follow the stages of the moon?"

And she would answer their many queries as well. Did she like to cook? Did she like to travel? What was her favorite music? All of which, she had determined, were thinly veiled questions about her marriageability and, ultimately, sex. A woman who can cook might like to roll around in whipped cream, for example, opening herself up to the ultimate food-sex experience for a man. A woman who likes to travel might be had on an ancient Roman aqueduct. A woman who likes Brahms likes it slow and steady, and without unnecessary flourish. She imagined men thinking these things as they asked her such mundane questions.

Or was she reading too much into them? She wasn't sure. What she was sure of was that she needed to find someone, and soon. She was pushing forty, a number she thought she could actually hear, in her head, whispering to her. "You are ready," it said, "ready for love." Magazines she read at the nail salon where she went for her biweekly pedicure called it the ticking of her biological clock. But Chloe thought it was much more like the whispering of the season and perhaps, also, of her grandmother, Rebecca Tziporra Goldstein, from across an ocean, where she lay buried in a graveyard outside the Lodz ghetto. As a fair-complected blond, she had "passed" for an Aryan and managed to escape the ghetto with some falsified papers to obtain a day job as a seamstress. She was residing with a non-Jewish family who had known her father, and there she had given birth to baby Solomon. Two days later, Nazi guards had appeared at the door of this family's house, and they'd taken Rebecca out into the courtyard and shot her. The shocked family hid the baby and, after the war, found some distant relatives in Cleveland.

Baby Sol was spirited away by relatives to the new world, to New York and eventually to Cleveland, where he grew into a smart boy who shined shoes, delivered newspapers, and eventually got a job writing for one, until one day he was anointed editor. At that point, at age fifty-two, he impregnated Chloe's mother, a cub reporter, twenty years his junior, one night when she was working late. Chloe was born to this young woman, out of wedlock, the following winter, and Solomon had appeared with a bouquet of white carnations the day following her birth, at the hospital. She would be his only child.

"Carnations?" asked Demetria Alejandra Lopez. "Aren't they for the dead?" She was appalled by the inappropriate choice of flowers on the occasion of her daughter's birth. In her family, such a thing might constitute a curse or even an omen.

"I didn't know," said Sol. "I am sorry." His eyes teared up and it was clear he was sorry for that and for many things. The way he had courted her with a lame-ass invitation to see the full moon rising over the parking lot. The coffee cup rings he had left on her beautiful, organized, and clean desk.

CONTENTS

"It's okay, Solomon," said Demetria, feeling suddenly sorry for him. He was older, after all, and would never be able to ask her to marry him, or anyone for that matter. He was a famous bachelor in the small Ohio town and drove a car that was flashy to the point of being unseemly, a silver Audi convertible. He had no taste in clothes. And he was balding. On the back of his head was a shiny crown of tanned flesh, like a yarmulke that had vacationed in Florida. She would never marry him, even if he asked. She had her hopes pinned on a man her own age named Marcos Eugenio Martinez, who owned an auto body repair shop that was known for its detailing jobs and the neat pinstripes and fancy flames they painted onto the sides of Camaros and Mustangs and Trans Ams. Demetria would marry Marcos a year later and have a succession of sons, Chloe's three wild and adventurous brothers. But she would always be the special one, the mystery *hija*, whose father was by then a wealthy Jewish newspaper publisher who paid for her to attend college at Barnard, where she had majored in art history.

"Your grandmother, my mother, Rebecca, would be so proud of you," he said to his only child, on the occasion of her college graduation. He had taken her out to Applebee's for a special celebration supper. He had ordered the Bourbon Street Steak, part of a new promotion they were having for meats cooked with liquor. She had ordered a Cobb salad. He insisted she order a second course, the roast chicken chipotle. "Indulge," he said. And when it arrived, shiny with glaze and steaming hot, he said to her: "Dig in."

At the end of the meal he had given her the keys to her very own car, a shiny new BMW convertible with red leather seats, like a cousin of his own car. She thanked him profusely, for everything: the college education, the car, the peppery chicken that glistened in its sauce. But the comment he had made, it was curious. It was the first she had ever heard of this grandmother. She and her father had not spent much time together over the years and rarely talked about much beyond the weather and her grades in school.

"Who was she? What was she like?" Chloe asked. In her other family, the ones who had actually raised her, fed her, told her to take better care of her kitten and brush her hair, grandmothers were very important people. There was Abuelita Rosa, on her stepfather's side, from Cuba, who made cinnamon cookies and could read palms, tea leaves, everything. "The sky says you will be a bride within six years," she would chant. "The dandelions say you will marry rich and be fruitful." And then there was Abuela Delilah, from Tijuana, who cooked and fed and cooked and fed, all her life, until she finally died, stirring a pot of her beloved red chili stew.

Who was this other *abuela*, this Polish woman, who might feel proud somewhere beyond this earth of her Barnard degree, freshly minted and pressed into its plastic and leather frame?

"I never knew my mother, but I know she would love you, as I do," Sol said. Chloe blushed at this confession of emotion, so unusual for her father, who usually spoke only in guarded and clinical sentences, giving advice about money and life. Once, coming upon a drawer of change in her apartment while looking for a fork, he actually said, "This isn't earning any interest in here."

"Dad," she said, "must you reinforce such tired stereotypes about race?"

"Alas," he said. "I must."

This was how they usually spoke to each other. In sentences full of ironic references and sardonic asides, which lightened up the sorry nature of their real-world relationship, the man who had never meant to be a father and the bastard daughter he had sired. A knack for playful irony is important in such situations.

With help from her father, and a micro loan from the government, Chloe had opened her own business and was quite successful. It was an art gallery with a companion shop, based on the theme of recycling. The sculpture she showed was art made of other things. A farmer who welded together old found farm implements. A woman who welded together egg beaters. On the other side she sold assorted items: ducks made of detergent bottles. A large wall hanging made of emptied tampon containers, painted black. It was called *Menopause*.

But the secret to her success had been the opening up of a large back room for "art birthday parties," which had gone over well in her community. She charged twenty dollars a child, and each one could make his or her choice of a painting, sculpture, or tie-dye tee shirt, with her help. She had colorful smocks in every size hanging in the window, with a sign that said "Celebrate Art."

It didn't hurt that her father had arranged for numerous feature articles on her business, some on the front page of the *Cleveland Herald*. He was a man who usually exhibited flawless business ethics, even if his sexual ethics had been a bit lacking. He had caught some flack for this indiscretion. But the same people who accused him later forgave him the trespass, as he made up for it with his expression of paternal support. And who could really, seriously condemn that? It was also, all agreed, an extremely original business model. Chloe was attractive, if a bit plump, or "a wee bit zaftig," as her father described it, and her gallery, ART PLAY, had become a very popular stopping place in town, for the frequent openings and art parties, readings, lectures, and slide shows she sponsored there. She had also begun a monthly free movie event, projected on the side of her 1899 white brick building. She set up seats in the parking lot and invited the public to see such eclectic fare as *The Maltese Falcon, Murder on the Orient Express*, and *Bambi*. The movie screenings were wildly popular in the neighborhood, which was a bit down on its heels and striving to be better, like a man who has just been let out of prison and has his first good, real job. A man who dresses very nicely and is on his best behavior, aiming to please. That was the sort of neighborhood where Chloe had her business. And her business, especially the film screenings, made it feel better about itself.

Yes, she thought each night as she checked the various online dating sites where she had posted, like a hunter checking traps. *I am a giver. I am fun. I am interesting and I have spectacular eyes. Someone will find me. Someone will love me.*

She really did have great eyes. They were green with a penchant to shift into blue-green at times, such as when she was preoccupied with something or wore a certain color sweater. Those eyes were the gift of her grandmother from Lodz.

It was on one of these occasions, checking her sites and postings, acting the huntress, when she found Ivan. He was thirty-six, medium height and build, and, as he put it, "handsome without being a Ken doll." She liked that phrase. It bespoke a sense of humor like her own. Sort of the way she and her father bantered.

Ivan lived in a nearby town and ran a print shop. He made signs, wedding invitations, and anything else people might need printed up. He used desktop publishing. He liked what he did, he said, because it involved words. Ivan was a closet poet, he confessed in one texting session that had bled into the early morning hours. He texted one of Romeo's soliloquies:

O, she doth teach the torches to burn bright!
It seems she hangs upon the cheek of night
Like a rich jewel in an Ethiope's ear;
Beauty too rich for use, for earth too dear!
So shows a snowy dove trooping with crows,
As yonder lady o'er her fellows shows.

Chloe felt her chest tighten. He had not only read but memorized something from Shakespeare. She had memorized almost all of *Hamlet*.

"Would you like to meet for dinner?" he had finally asked, during another late-night texting session. "Saturday night? Ground Round?"

Yes, yes, yes! she thought, but soberly typed out, "Sure." She had read in a magazine that it wasn't good to sound too eager. She would bring along some promotional pamphlets about ART PLAY for him to display in his print shop, aptly called the Print Shoppe. "Why the extra 'p' and 'e'?" Chloe had asked Ivan, during one of their first online chats.

"It is a play for cuteness. Or quaintness. Or antiqueness. Some kind of ness," he wrote back. It was such a winning answer, so honest and slyly self-deprecating. And clever. It was clever. She was falling in love with his online persona, she thought. *And autumn is here,* she thought, looking out the window at the browning grass, covered in twisty seeds dropped by her Japanese mimosa tree, *the true season for love.* She noted it again, the way everything, everywhere was making a last bid for reproduction. Sending out one last batch of embryos into the world, like postcards to unknown lovers. Would a love seed take somewhere and implant, grow and thrive?

As their date approached, Chloe found herself growing fonder of Ivan. *I think it might even be something like love,* she wrote to her friend Cassandra, who had briefly been her roommate at Barnard until she dropped out to marry Hans, a sax player from Berlin. The two had had many adventures and traveled the world for an entire year; Chloe had received postcards from Melbourne, Addis Ababa, Cinque Terre, and Montreal. They had become her model for true love. They dispatched sentences like, "Marvelous bananas here in Islamorada!" and "Stupendous sunsets in Truth or Consequences!" She asked Ivan what he thought of travel. "Never thought much about it," he replied, "though I do love Disney. Joking."

She loved that: the word "joking."

As the day drew near, the fall seemed to fragment into pieces. There was a flurry of leaves, flowers letting loose final frantic handfuls of seeds. Leaf dust coating the sidewalks, getting up into your eyes even. The cottonwoods released great gobs of white fluff, like warm snow.

Chloe imagined that at night, when she was sleeping, the animals would come out of their holes and burrows and enact elaborate courtship rituals, swing wildly into one another's paws from the treetops, waltzing in the parking lots.

Soon I will meet Ivan, and we will eat dinner together at Ground Round. We will speak in ironic, sardonic phrases. And maybe, when he walks me to my car, we will kiss.

She thought the animals would desist their dancing and courtship to look on at the human version, the way she often watched them, the squirrels hopping off the tree branches or mad dashing toward one another across a telephone wire. The deer peeking from the brush behind her house, shyly. Finally, it would happen; the animals would be watching *her*.

She'd had exactly seven boyfriends in her life, and four had been in college. The other three had been introductions made by her brothers (all of whom were happily married with children), to their friends. Men with names like Eugenio (a construction worker), Milan (owned a pizza joint in her neighborhood), and Miguel (a mysterious source of money—Chloe suspected he grew hydroponic marijuana in the basement of his gaudy McMansion in the outskirts of Cleveland). Nothing wrong with these men, no, not at all, perfectly cordial, dressed well, good-looking and all that, but there was no sense of wonder there for her, no light electric shock traveling down her spine when their numbers showed up on her cell phone, no light-headed feeling when they came to her door. Ivan, on the other hand, had inspired all of the above, and they hadn't even met.

Chloe had one of her rare coffee dates with her father, and when he asked his usual question—"Seeing anyone special, or not so special, or even completely boring?"—she decided to tell him about Ivan. Their date was two days away.

"Well, sort of, I think I am in love," she said, "a bit," enjoying the effect it had on her dad. He sat upright and looked intensely interested. Love, he thought, was a sensation he had never felt. He had experienced lust, attraction, and desire numerous times, but love was a foreign country. Like Poland, it seemed distant and full of danger. So far away from anywhere he had ever been. "In love!" he said. "Like on television."

"Yes," said Chloe, "just like that."

"Well . . . tell me all about it," Sol said.

"He runs a print shop," she said. "He likes sushi. He hikes. And he's funny. What more could I ask for?"

"Hmm . . ." said Sol, touching his temple with his index finger. "Now that I think about it, eats sushi, hikes, is employed, that about covers it. I think you should marry him."

"I plan to," said Chloe, smiling back at him, with her Lodz grandmother's eyes, shifting between green and blue. They ordered chocolate cake, for dessert. A rare indulgence that felt like a sort of sugar bargain struck between them. A deal made. A closing argument in the country of desserts. Chloe and Ivan. Yes.

Her three brothers and their wives teased her mercilessly when she came home for a dinner one night with their combined families. "Chloe and Ivan sittin' in a tree. K-I-S-S-I-N-G. First comes love, then comes marriage, then comes Chloe with a baby carriage!" They pronounced his name ee-Van, the "van" rhyming with "lawn," the Hispanic version. Her father had pronounced it with a distinctly Yiddish flair. She had no idea how to actually pronounce it, as she had only seen it written. Ivan could be anyone. He could be anything. An exotic and burly Russian. He could have a ballet dancer's physique. All she knew was he was anglo and had a nice smile. That was from one fuzzy picture he had posted online. It could be a very, very old photograph. It was definitely out of focus. Odd, she thought, for a man who ran a print shop and must have a very good eye for visual clarity.

Two days later, Chloe sifted through her closet for something to wear. Something casual but not unattractive. No, gorgeous without seeming intentionally so. Something utterly lovely but haphazard-ish. Could such an outfit exist? It was like looking for a rare bird in a familiar forest. You know she might be there, somewhere, lurking, and once you found her you would say, of course, *Little special breed of starling, I knew you were there all along!* But until you spot her she is altogether missing. Maybe even extinct, a dodo bird. Buried and fossilized beneath the dirty laundry.

Finally she located it, a thrift store find, a gauzy white and rose floral blouse, a teensy bit see-through. Suggestive yet traditional, sexy yet austere, with its formal collar and slight ruffle up the front. Was it prissy? With her Levi's that were nicely worn in and fit just right over her slightly generous rear (what her dad called her *tuchus deluxe*) ("DAD!" she would smile and say. "It is highly inappropriate to address your daughter thusly.") ("Yes, sorry about that," he'd say.) (Could there be such a thing as flirtation between a father and daughter, an utterly asexual banter of fun?).

As she got in her car and drove to the restaurant, Chloe's heart pounded. She pulled in to a parking space and walked inside, looking for a man who seemed like he could be named Ivan. A man who had dark hair and an ironic smile. Nobody approached her. Everyone seemed as if they were already paired up and had been assigned seating. People were in family units, with baby car seat carriers in tow and daughters in matching dresses. No single man in the lot. No Ivan-ish creature lurking in the shadows.

She sat down at the bar, with her back to the door, and ordered a lemonade. Good to order a nonalcoholic beverage and then take her cue from Ivan about what to order next. You never know what people are like. He could be anti-alcohol. Or a recovering alcoholic. Or simply someone who mildly disapproves of alcohol. Chloe thought this would not be a good thing, particularly, and would bespeak a certain stiffness of character. Oh, she was thinking way, way too much.

She kept glancing behind her to see if anyone had come in, an Ivan-ish someone. Perhaps with a mustache, though she hoped he had not grown one, as she hated them. More families with children. More people in pairs, people holding hands, people dressed similarly, as if they had been living together such a long time they had melded closets. Morphed tastes. These were the people she was trying to become, she thought. These were the chosen ones. The coupled. The people who had found love. But they looked pretty unhappy, or bored, or somehow unpleasant to her.

Maybe this was a mistake, this online love search. She felt her skin prickle. He was fifteen minutes late. Chloe glanced behind her and saw a man walk in. He had a cane and some sort of unpleasant hat on, not a bowler exactly, but something like one. He was twenty pounds overweight and wore thick Coke-bottle glasses. He had on (oh was it really?) a gold chain necklace and his shirt was unbuttoned way too far. He surveyed the room, whisking right past her.

What Ivan saw was a plumpish woman at a bar, wearing an unbecoming shirt that was unpleasantly risqué, see-through even. How brash, how forward, how even a little desperate, he thought. She was drinking, too, probably an alcoholic drink. Or maybe she was drinking water. No, it looked like a drink. *She was probably a drunk.*

The woman at the bar headed for the back door to make a hasty escape just as he pivoted on his heels to flee in the other direction. Somehow, the two managed to walk right into each other in the parking lot. Each one was looking behind them, nervously, when they collided. "Oh, excuse me, sir," Chloe said, her heart pounding. "I didn't mean to bump into you." His left eye was milky. An eye that had gone wrong somehow, or had contracted some rare left-eye disease.

"No problem," muttered the man. "It was my fault. Really! I wasn't paying attention." He glanced at her slightly wide rear, the fronds of disheveled curly black hair circling her face. They both trotted quickly to their vehicles, which were parked, unpleasantly, next to each other.

Then, as Ivan got into his truck, he caught a glimpse of her blue-green eyes. *Enchanting somehow*, he thought, *but too late. I have made my exit*, he thought. She caught a glimpse of him looking at her and something flashed in her heart. *There goes my beloved,* she thought sarcastically, *my husband who never was.*

They each peeled out of the parking lot a little too fast, Ivan making an unpleasant squeal with the tires of his circa 1998 Ford Explorer. Chloe letting her foot hit the gas on the BMW convertible her father had given her with a pop, so it seemed to leap into the oncoming traffic like an anxious deer, or a rabbit that had been dancing too long and had forgotten how to move at a normal pace.

At a traffic light they somehow ended up side by side. *Oh no*, she thought, he was rolling down his window. He was signaling to her to roll down her window. She did so, reluctantly.

"Chloe," the man said, looking suddenly, surprisingly debonair and attractive despite the milky eye and bowler, the gold chain, the shirt that desperately needed buttoning. He looked good at that moment in a sort of downtrodden, been-there-and-done-that-and-seen-the-world way, like a Tom Waits–ish character, who had been down on his luck but survived the wiser. And the bowler was daring really, when you thought about it. "Is that you?"

She nodded and he found himself enjoying the unpretentious way she did so, and her hair, with its wildness, was somehow appealing. The gauzy shirt alluring. "Pull into Starbucks," he said, signaling to the next corner. "Let's talk."

Chloe felt her heart start up, a drum kit that had been turned off all summer, flicked suddenly on.

A breeze from the rolled-down window grazed her arm as she followed Ivan's truck into the parking lot. It smelled like burning leaves and mulch, the last scents of a dying summer. The smell of happy backyards where families were raking up, making piles for their children to jump in, which the children would then do with a certain palpable abandon, roaring with laughter. That beautiful thing children do before they realize other people might be watching, and they tone it down, pare it back, and begin to become the people they will be in the world as adults. All the while the animals look on, wondering how they do it, and why.

Death by Free Verse

After two months of exchanging pleasantries, of back-and-forth flirting, of this and that–ing, zig and zagging, chit and chatting online, Myra suggested Louis and she meet.

"I am getting ready for midterms," he wrote back (he was a college professor). "Bad timing."

Okay, truth: It stung a little, to have put one's heart out there and to have had it slapped back by some college scheduling protocol. But Myra did not give up easily.

Louis was intriguing. He had climbed trees in Sri Lanka and had spent a good deal of time on an elephant preserve. He had sent some pictures of himself hanging upside down from a branch over an elephant's head.

"You are jungley," she had written.

"I am jungley," he wrote back.

Much of their correspondence had taken the form of limericks:

There was a young man in Colombo
who liked to play chess with Dumbo
He sat on her trunk
In a terrible funk
Her checkmates had made him quite humble.

"But 'humble' doesn't actually rhyme with 'dumbo,'" he said.

"Picky, picky," she replied.

Then he wrote one to her:

There was a poetess from Kent
Who wrote limericks which she sent
She had a gift for rhyme
(well, most of the time)
Though her humor was terribly bent.

"Bent? My humor is bent? Are you saying you don't like my jokes?"

"No," he replied, "I couldn't think of anything else to rhyme with 'Kent.'"

"How about 'went,' 'lent,' 'rent,' or for that matter, 'elephant,' which would be a slant rhyme, of course."

"What is a slant rhyme?"

"A half rhyme, an off rhyme."

"Sounds like a cheating rhyme to me," he said.

Sometimes, late at night, their limerick texts had taken a more serious turn. They had written passionately about what they looked for in love, and in another person.

"What is it you seek, Louis? Love, lust, friendship, other?"

"Love is lovely," he wrote back; "lust can get sticky but is ultimately worth it; friendship can be community-building; and other, hmmm . . . I guess I would like to meet someone who can cook. More. Than. Spaghetti."

Apparently Louis's ex had made nothing but spaghetti.

"I cook," wrote Myra. "It just so happens I cook very well."

"What do you cook?"

"I cook brisket, Moroccan lamb stew, shrimp Alfredo, and Thai, I cook Thai. I have several recipes. Like chicken satay."

"You make chicken satay?" he texted. "I may have to marry you."

"Okay," she wrote back. "I accept."

Louis had just returned from a three-week trek in the Golden Triangle region, where he had gone white-water rafting and smoked opium with a village chief.

"Why is it everyone I know who has been trekking in Thailand has smoked opium with a village chief?" Myra asked.

"Oh, it is part of the standard trek package," Louis replied. Louis was funny.

When Louis declined the invitation to have lunch somewhere, Myra decided to confront his reticence with another limerick.

There once was a man who liked girls
but his love life began to unfurl
So he made reservations
To visit distant nations
To find happiness, diamonds, and pearls.

"Okay," Louis wrote, "that was a stretch."

"What? The rhymes? Or don't you like girls?"

"No, I am pretty sure I like girls. The whole jewelry trope."

"I know," Myra wrote back. "I was at a loss for words."

"A good time NOT to write a limerick."

"Says he of 'bent' humor."

"Touché."

"Okay, we are even, but I still think we should have lunch," Myra wrote.

"Send me some pictures," he texted, quite out of the blue.

"I sent you pictures," she wrote.

"But they are just head shots . . ."

"Louis, are you asking me to send you nude pix?"

"NO, just something that shows you, the real you."

Myra was stumped. She had sent him pictures. But he wanted more, so she sent more. She sent him one of her rowing her kayak and one of her standing in front of her kayak.

With the photos she sent him another limerick.

This is my kayak, Lenore
She's a skiff you might love and adore
She is small, sleek, and fun
In her, rapids you can run
and her owner invites you for more.

Immediately came his response—just one word, but oh such an important one:

"More?"

"Yes, more, like lunch."

"You are cute," he wrote. "I think you are pretty."

"And I think you are cute too. I will be honest, I am smitten."

"Smitten?"

"Smitten."

Silence for two days was followed by the following dispatch from Louis to Myra.

I think I am in love with you, Myra
And I think I might like to come try ya
We can drive in my car

To some very small bar
Where we might like to have some papaya.

"Okay," Myra wrote back. "That was clever."

Her smittenness had gotten quite out of control. She was thinking about Louis pretty much all the time. She woke up and thought about him and then went to work and thought about him. She kept returning to the photo of him hanging from that tree in Sri Lanka. In fact, it seemed a little stalker-y, but she actually made that photograph into her screen saver.

When she came home at night she practiced recipes for Thai fare to prepare for their courtship. She learned how to make a lemongrass soup and several tasty curry dishes.

Then Myra wrote a beautiful love poem. It might have been the most beautiful love poem ever written, she thought. (And Myra was an actual poet. An MFA-degree-carrying, poetry-teaching poet who worked with the Connecticut "Poetry in the Schools" program. She had credentials.) Her love poem had three sections. It was full of winning metaphors and synonyms. It had great images. But most important, it had heart. Real heart.

To send it or not to send it? That was the question. She pondered it all night long, and then finally at 2:00 a.m. she did it. She pushed the button. She sent the poem.

Here is the love poem that Myra sent Louis:

YES, DUDE, A LOVE POEM

I

Tonight I will be the traveler of you.
I will travel the valleys and hills of you,
the faraway deserts of you,
I will drink from the rivers and streams of you
I will backpack through your high terrain,
where I will get dizzy from the altitude,
I will go above your timber line
I will find the beautiful places
that make me swoon.
I will go to all the places you recommend
and some you have forgotten.
I will travel you without a map
or compass, I will navigate
by the stars and the moon,
the planet we live on,
my own bones, they will tell me
how to crawl inside your laughter
and I will sleep there.

II

Tonight I will be the student of you.
I will study the smallest
and the greatest parts of you,

the lines and crannies of you,
the little accidents of you.
Your scars and your muscles,
your skin and hips.
I will study the small country of each hand
isthmus of neck, the great plains of your back
I will follow your numbers, research your skin,
learn your mouth, your eyes
There is an algebra of you
and I will solve for x.

III

Tonight I will be the professor of you.
I will teach you the ways of me,
the backroads, the unseen of me,
I will show you the how and the why
and the where of me,
places I have not been in a long time
and maybe never been.
I will take you to the lakes of me,
the full harvest moon
of me, the secrets of me,
the known of me,
I will show you the long toothed scar
on my left foot
where they opened me up
and sewed me back,

In fact, I will show you all the places
I have been broken
and healed again,
my blessings
and my wounds,
the gifts of me, the solaces,
the carnival ride of me,
the candy of me,
the light of me in the dark.

So, after she sent this poem, as you might imagine, Myra felt a little vulnerable. It had not been a limerick or anything like a limerick. It was not a poem with a joke in it or a joke with a poem in it. It was a serious real-life love poem. But then he had said he was in love with her, right? Or was he being flip? Three weeks went by.

We repeat here (and italicize) for emphasis: *three weeks*. No return e-mail from Louis.

"Ummm. Hi?" she finally wrote. "Sorry if you hated my poem."

Still nothing. "Umm, wow, you really hated it."

Finally, a Louis message appeared in her in-box.

It was this:

"Been busy. Lots of stuff with my job. Going on a quick backpacking trip to Senegal."

Senegal? Quick? Like really? she thought.

Finally, stumped beyond stumped, she wrote to her best friend, Lenore (yes, she for whom her kayak had been named). Lenore was a playwright and poet who lived in Manhattan and the smartest cookie around. She "knew from relationships," she liked to say, and was a huge yenta, fixing up everyone they knew, successfully, for years.

"Lenore, help," Myra e-mailed.

"Not the limerick guy still," Lenore wrote back.

"Yes, that very one. So would you believe it if some guy told you he was going to Senegal?"

"Hmmm, Senegal," wrote Lenore. "Is he a diplomat?"

"No."

"Aid worker?"

"No."

"Does he work for an NGO or for Doctors Without Borders?"

"No," wrote Myra. "Backpacking."

"Then no, the answer is no, I would not believe a guy who said he was going to Senegal to go backpacking. I think they might be having a civil war. Or are about to have one. Or just finished one up."

"That is what I was afraid of."

"So tell me," Lenore wrote, "what did you do?"

"Nothing! I sent him a poem."

"Limerick?"

"No."

"Don't tell me you sent him a sonnet. You must never send a sonnet before the first date."

"It wasn't a sonnet."

"A villanelle, then?"

"Nope."

"Not a pantoum—please tell me you didn't send him a pantoum!"

"It wasn't a pantoum. By the way, I hate pantoums."

"Me, too. I think everyone hates pantoums."

"Well it wasn't a pantoum."

"So what, then? What did you send him?"

"I sent him a free verse poem. A love poem."

"Oh, honey," Lenore wrote. "Not free verse."

"What?"

"A free verse love poem? Tell me it wasn't in sections."

"It was. It had three sections."

"Kiss of death, babe."

"Apparently."

At this point Lenore shared the Rules for Poetry When Dating Online. Clever, short iambic pentameter poems with no more than two verses are okay before the first date, as are haiku, limericks, and tanka. No sonnets, villanelle, or pantoums until at least three dates have gone by successfully. As for free verse love poems, save those for a one-year anniversary, she said.

"Is this like a credo?" Myra asked.

"It's a doctrine," Lenore wrote back.

Myra had killed her flirtation with Louis with sectioned free verse. It was sad and because it was sad she had to appropriately mourn it. To do so she spent a week in bed eating Häagen-Dazs Rum Raisin ice cream, after which she switched to Ben & Jerry's Cherry Garcia.

About a year went by and Myra's affection for Louis cooled. In fact, it had gone extinct, like the woolly mammoths, receding to a small set of bones buried somewhere deep down inside her. Over drinks in Manhattan with Lenore, Myra said yes, she had truly learned her lesson this time.

"The Love Poetry Doctrine is not to be messed with," Lenore said.

"I get it. Anyway he was a liar. He said he was going backpacking in Senegal. Remember? That was a lie."

"Wait," said Lenore. "Senegal?"

"Yes, Senegal . . ."

One year earlier, Myra had finally Googled "travel" and "Senegal" to learn that:

> This advice has been reviewed and reissued with an amendment to the Travel Summary and the Safety and Security—Terrorism section (there is an underlying threat from terrorism). The overall level of the advice has not changed; we continue to advise against road travel in the Casmance region to the west of Kolda.

"I think I read something about some guy traveling in Senegal who was abducted last year, near Kolda," Lenore said.

"You are joking," said Myra. "Tell me you don't think that's funny."

"What if it's your limerick guy?"

The question settled in Myra's gut like a stone. What if? Myra thought about this possibility all the way back to Connecticut on the train.

The woolly mammoth fossilized in her heart had been awakened and was trumpeting around. It was smashing things. It was making a big mess.

For the entire next week, she couldn't sleep. What if Louis was rotting in some Senegalese terror camp? She had to know. She couldn't sleep. In fact, she had stooped to the level of nightly Excedrin PMs. It was a problem. She tried to switch to valerian root tea, but the stuff didn't even touch her insomnia.

Finally, she decided to write to Louis. It wouldn't be stalker-y if she wrote to him one last time (he need never know about the screen saver thing, which had long been replaced by a stock photo of a sunset). This is what she wrote:

Dear Louis,
I am not trying to bother you. You disappeared and it was your right to do so. But I am a bit worried about you. I understand if my poem was upsetting and you decided to ditch me for the crime of sucky poetry. I even approve. But if you are in trouble somewhere (like, say, Senegal, which is where you were going

when last we communicated), or need something or if
there is some other reason you never wrote me back
after I sent my poem, please let me know. As a cour-
tesy. I don't like to think about you rotting in some
hole in Senegal.
Sincerely,
Myra

Two weeks later, she did hear back from Louis. It was
the last time she heard from him.

There once was a young divorcé
Who liked to eat chicken satay
After travel in Senegal
With his very best pal
He realized, in fact, he was gay.

People Who Live Far, Far Away

Miko was an Icelandic yak farmer who was thirty-one years old and in possession of a small fortune.

Misty was twenty-three, an aspiring poet and model who lived in New York City and Beverly Hills, who'd had a small part as an extra in *Dude, Where's My Car?* You may recall her as the girl with the long blonde hair, long blonde legs—long blonde everything, in fact—who walks by right after the opening credits.

"It is a truth universally acknowledged that a young yak farmer, in possession of a large yak fortune, should be in pursuit of a wife," Misty said to her friend Blanche, with whom she was discussing her recent online dalliances.

"Say what?" said Blanche.

"That is an adaptation from *Pride and Prejudice,*" Misty said.

"Oh," said Blanche. "Well, I guess I just think Iceland is sorta far away."

"But that is exactly what makes it exciting," Misty said.

Several of Misty's friends from college, including Blanche, had recently gotten married and pregnant, and she had been experiencing some anxiety about it. She felt, for lack of a better phrase, left behind, as they all hung out at the Laundromat, folding adorable baby outfits, talking about what, exactly, might be the best brands of pacifiers, strollers, or teething rings. A cool Icelandic dude who likes nature and animals might be just the ticket, she thought, coming across Miko's profile on Matchhearts.com. He would be exotic enough to impress her friends, who, after college, had all so promptly given birth. The luckiest of them had married actors, writers, online game designers, or Wall Street guys. They gave their babies the most interesting names, like Thesis, Harmony, and Theorem. It was as if these babies had been brought into the world to figure out something big, like math or the way to write opera. In a world with such ambitious baby-making going on, it felt quite pathetic to be babyless, not to mention husbandless. Miko would be exotic enough to be cute. He would not be a wimp. How could a farmer of yaks be a wimp? He would be sweet and grateful to meet an actor-poet girl like herself who lived in New York City.

This was what Misty thought about late at night, after several apple martinis and a long walk home across Manhattan's west side. She lived in a walk-up, above an

S&M parlor, and she didn't like to get home too late because she risked encountering the bloodied patrons, heading for home. If she got there before eleven it would still be all quiet on the western front, as her best friend, Yoni, liked to say. He called her place the western front because it was really far west on the island of Manhattan, near the Meatpacking District, which Yoni, who was gay, seemed to think was a funny name, for reasons she did not truly comprehend but was afraid to ask about, as it might reveal her naiveté.

Miko seemed utterly exotic, in a refreshing way. Refreshing like Fresca, like the first snow of the year, like Icees. Just his name, Miko, was refreshing. She had never met a Miko.

Miko, for his part, was excited to meet a girl who had been in a Hollywood movie, in any capacity at all. He had seen *Dude, Where's My Car?* and thought it was very funny. He thought he recalled that girl in the opening scene, but he would have to get the movie again off Netflix and really look for her.

For the record, Miko did not really live in Iceland. Neither was he a yak farmer. It was just something he tried out to see if it would attract girls, which it obviously had. Call it a whim.

All of this was before the recent hullabaloo with the Icelandic volcano, when all the flights in Europe were grounded, when the whole world had seemed to come to a screeching halt, all because of ash.

"What do you mean, you have never heard of Eyjaf-jallajökull?" Misty asked. "It is right there on your continent. At least I think you live on a continent, or is it a very large island?"

"It is an island, for the record, but it is very big and not everyone knows the name of every single volcano on it."

"But isn't Eyjafjallajökull very large? And potentially dangerous?" They were talking on the phone at this point, in addition to e-mailing and texting, and Misty was sort of proud she had learned how to pronounce the name of the volcano, and she had learned it specifically to impress Miko. Yet here he didn't even know where it was.

Whether because of or despite their exotic identities, there was some suspicion on the part of each of these two young people, about the claims of the other. Even though there had been no explosion in their lives, let's just say they had each been burned.

"I am a yak farmer. Ask me something—in fact ANYTHING—about yaks and I will answer. I do not know much about volcanoes."

"Okay, what do yaks eat?" Misty ventured.

"They eat grass. Hay. Twigs. Stuff that grows," Miko answered. "Now tell me again which is you in that movie?" *Why* did she insist on talking about obscure volcanoes?

Misty was annoyed. Why did he insist on talking about her role in *Dude, Where's My Car?*

For the record, Misty had not really been in that movie. She just wrote that in her profile to attract interest, which it obviously had.

"So watchya wearing?" Miko asked.

"Nothing," Misty replied. "What are you wearing?"

"Not much more."

"That's nice. Okay, I have to go now," she said.

For some reason she felt annoyed. This was not the cool, exotic foreign-man experience she signed up for. He barely had an accent. And the accent he did have was like someone she once knew from Cleveland.

Miko hung up the phone. His name was actually Mark. He was pissed. This Misty was not the person she had represented herself as. An actress who played an extra in the first scene of *Dude, Where's My Car?* should be up for at least a tad of phone sex.

A week later Misty, bored, wrote to "Miko" again. "Hi, how is it going? How are the yaks?"

"I am a police officer in Akron," he wrote back. "Like some yak farmer is going to have access to the Internet. What are you, stupid?" He was sick of this crap.

"Oh really, officer? Well, you should get a ticket for lying."

"What about you? Tell me you didn't lie. I rented *Dude, Where's My Car?* There is no blonde in the opening scene."

"Touché," she typed.

"So who are you, then?"

"A waitress on Pier 17."

"Where is that?"

"New York City."

"Really? That is kinda cool."

"Hardly," she wrote.

She flicked off her computer.

Two weeks later, Mark got an instant message from Misty. Utterly lonely one night, she wrote to him again. "Actually, I do like men in uniforms. Send a picture?"

A picture of a handsome cop zinged onto her screen.

"Cute!"

"And do I get to see one of you?"

An adorable woman in a waitress uniform appeared in a flash.

"Very pretty."

"So are you going to arrest me, officer, for lying?"

"Not if you bring me some dessert, waitress. But it better be sweet."

In this manner they flirted for two nights, waitress and police officer, apron and badge, dessert tray and handcuffs. Instant messages flinging through the ether, practically singeing their screens.

Alas, Mark was not a police officer. He was a veteran, who had been paralyzed from the waist down by an explosive device in Afghanistan. He lived with his parents in Duluth.

Alas, not only was Misty not a poet and actress, but she was also not a waitress. She was the caretaker of her twin sister, Mandy, who had severe Down syndrome. She lived in a teensy apartment that had belonged to their grandparents. Although she had been an English major at NYU, she now spent her days wiping up spilled drinks, spoon-feeding her sister, and changing her Depends. Once a week she got a person from "caregiver respite" to watch Mandy so she could go out and get drunk with Yoni or hang out with Blanche and the girls she knew from the Laundromat on the corner. She was a fag hag. That is what her girlfriends called her. She was a laundry chick. That was Yoni's name for her. Whatever she was, it was distinctly unglamorous. Even less glamorous than a waitress. Which is pretty bad, when you think about it.

Her days were long and tedious, and sometimes even a little gross. Her sister would toss her food onto the floor. She would pull Mandy's hair at times. Caring for her was a thankless task she did because she felt it was *the right thing to do.*

The sound of the chime on her laptop, signaling an instant message from Mark, would interrupt these long days. It sounded like the opening note of a symphony, the sound of another life calling, of options, of the reversal of her rather cumbersome credit card debt. It was the sound of planets whizzing around in distant solar systems. And even though she knew it wasn't real, it somehow still recalled an image of a man in some icy expanse, herding yaks.

The buzz of Mark's iPhone, on receiving Misty's instant message, would often jolt him from a nap he was taking in a corner of his parents' living room, with the television droning away in the background, some talk show or soap opera his mother liked to leave on while she did her housework. So she wasn't an actress or a waitress or whatever; the buzz of his phone with her name appearing on the screen was still the sound that he thought sunshine would make if it made a sound. It was the sound that feet made, walking across a room. The sound of walking itself. Of movement. Of *before*.

And sometimes, still, even though he knew it wasn't so, it was the sound of a blonde, leggy actress, walking across the credit screen of *Dude, Where's My Car?* Walking confidently and with a sexy waggle, toward the edge of the screen, to a place where he could see her perfectly. Where somehow, amazingly, she could also see him.

Life Underground

The Happily Ever After sat on a shelf and stared down at Alana. It had made itself quite at home right there in her kitchen, on the little shelf above the sink.

It sat there smugly, in that family portrait of her sister Brianna, brother-in-law Peter, and their 2.5 kids (little Megan still in the oven then), all smiling, in some forest somewhere, doing happy, foresty things. Things that necessitated bungee cords and really good hiking boots purchased from the L.L.Bean catalog.

Every time she cooked a dish, it smirked at her a bit.

She saw the Happily Ever After in the grocery store, too. Couples with their babies strapped on in very cool Swedish baby carriers, consulting about avocado condition or debating, so seriously, like delegates at a UN convention: asparagus or brussels sprouts? Pine nuts or almonds?

She prickled at the warmth of it; you could feel it even down the aisle. The Happily Ever After had its own internal combustion engine. You could probably warm yourself just by sitting next to it on a cold day, or even tan a bit. It was so incredible how it seemed wholly devoid of angst. Faces flushed with that joy that comes from having to worry only about which flavor of yogurt to try or whether to have a gluten-free breakfast or indulge in a few carbs. That love thing completely taken care of.

Although she felt fairly content in life—she was grateful for the independence and creativity that her lucrative work designing websites afforded her and really loved the Saturday-afternoon yoga class she taught at the health club—Alana couldn't help thinking it might be nice to have a Happily Ever After of her own. And, for the first time in years, there was some real potential on the horizon, since she'd met Max.

Max appeared quite debonair on his Compassion atesingles.com webpage. In a recognizable brand of very good cycling gear, on a road beside the ocean, he stood astride his top-notch racing bicycle, a soft breeze rippling his slightly long, slightly disheveled black hair. He was fit and strong-looking, yet he had a face that appeared warm and inviting, a face that you wanted to fold into your life like an egg white, make a part of the whole cake of you. And he seemed so willing to provide a Happily Ever After for her. After all, it was he who found her!

"I wasn't actually a member here, but I saw your profile and had to join just to meet you," he wrote. "I couldn't get your beautiful face out of my head."

Okay, let's just take a moment to breathe deeply and seriously look at that sentence again, as Alana did:

I couldn't get your beautiful face out of my head.

He had written to her in that first dispatch that he *could not believe* she liked Tom Waits, too. Such a coincidence: "I am also a huge fan," he wrote. "I love the rawness and fury of his craggy voice. I even like the songs with the most unorthodox rhythms. They remind me of a rattly old truck driving down the road."

To think, he had written, that there was this beautiful woman who also liked Tom Waits—*what were the chances?*

As she had sat before her computer screen and stared at the message, then flipped back to his picture on the bike and the other pictures: Max next to his koi pond; Max on a boat, a warm glow of late sun napping on his shoulders; and Max at dusk, a pleasant-shaped shadow sleeping softly on his cheek.

Guilty pleasure: She toggled Max's photographs for days.

When it came to writing back, she was very terse. One sentence, cherry-picked words. When he asked her if she liked the woods (he had a thirty-acre spread he "enjoyed hiking around in"), she wrote back: "Love woods."

When he asked if she liked nature and mountains and rivers, she replied: "All of the above."

The reason she had kept her answers so clipped was that she didn't want to write anything to spoil it all. She had learned from experience that the slightest turn of phrase could puncture and deflate an online flirtation. And here it was: a Happily Ever After that had come right to her door. Well, her virtual door, anyway. It was so precious. But so delicate. After all, it had just come; it could also just disappear.

One wrong move, one wrong word, one wrong step and she could scare that Happily Ever After clean away. So Alana was cautious. Uber-cautious, in fact. She took her time and she was careful. Like a person who wants to pet a silky rabbit that has mysteriously stopped for a moment in a field, she inched very slowly forward. She knew it could bolt.

Okay, so it wasn't a real Happily Ever After; she couldn't frame it and send it to her sister or place it on *her* kitchen shelf, for example. But it was a damn good thing and better than anything she had had in a long, long time and frankly, she wanted, really wanted, to keep it.

Potential Max.

That night, she had another message from Max, a bright-red check mark on her home page.

"Just so you know, Alana, I am a really handy guy. I have built three houses; one of them is an underground house. I can fix anything, so just let me know if you have anything you need fixed."

She sat there before her computer screen looking at it: Potential Max had offered to potentially fix real things for her.

He had built an underground house! She let the idea of an underground house sidestroke into her imagination. If she and Max were together that would mean she could, potentially of course, live underground, or at least visit occasionally!

Alana had never been in an underground house or even given much thought to underground houses or even being underground for a good long time, but now the idea of an underground house was with her all the time, fully embedded. Sitting in the park, over her bag lunch, she imagined peering out of the side of a hill like a hobbit in Middle-earth. Life in a grass-covered knoll. It would be so cozy to live underground, not to mention safe. If people didn't know your house was there, right underneath them, they would be so much less likely to rob you. And don't forget the environmental aspect; it would be so green to live that way, literally.

Then Alana remembered: She had drawn a map of an underground city when she was a child. There were streets, supermarkets, a gym, a swimming pool area, apartments, and multiple levels of "under" with an underground elevator you could use to get lower and lower down. She had gotten the idea for the drawing after her family visited Carlsbad Caverns, on a vacation in southern New Mexico, where they actually took an elevator down inside the earth. The guide on the cave tour took her family and the tour group, room by room, into the innermost cavern chambers by the beam of an industrial-strength flashlight. Finally they had to crawl a bit to enter one last room, where the whole group stood in total darkness.

"Now, look in front of you, hold out your hand," the tour guide instructed. Alana, then nine, had held out her hand. Her sister Bree, beside her, just seven at the time, had whimpered: "I'm scared." She'd caught Bree's hand and held it tight, whispering to her: "It's okay, it's fun. We're invisible!"

"Hold your right hand in front of your face," the guide instructed.

She did.

"Wiggle your fingers."

She did.

"You can't see your hand at all, can you, or anything in this room . . . That is because right now you are in complete, total darkness; there's not one drop of light in here. You won't experience this again, because up there above, you are never in this kind of darkness. This is real darkness, actual darkness, rare in our world."

Then the guide snapped his fingers, and well-concealed colored lights snapped back at him from above, revealing a gorgeous, nearly baroque scene, brightly lit stalagmites and stalactites, crystals gleaming from the ceiling, bejeweled walls. They were standing in a jewelry box, a treasure trove of sparkling light. But Alana would always remember thinking that the real treasure was the darkness that the room had held before: not fake but *real* dark.

She answered Max's note carefully, in the sparsest of prose:

"It is great to be handy and be able to fix things. An underground house sounds lovely; I imagine it as very safe and tight, cool in the summer and warm in the winter."

The days went on and Alana felt better and better about life, about herself, everything. She carried the thought of Max, whom she still hadn't met, around with her like a secret. To the store, to the bank, to the gym. She had a potential mate. He could even fix things in her house, like that leaky pipe in the basement. But she dared not really ask him to fix it, because to do so might somehow mar this fragile connection they had going. And she loved this slipknot of affection they were tying with their typed words; she looked forward to the missives and the promise they held of real-world interactions in some future someday.

Max seemed excited about her, too:

"In the summer I can show you all around the mountains on my Harley. There is no better way to see the Adirondacks than on the back of a Harley!"

"I am very creative," he wrote on another evening. "I could make things for you in stained glass."

Having a potential gift of stained glass was almost as good as a real gift of stained glass, maybe even better, Alana thought, as real stained glass might break. It was such a lovely thing that Alana thought about it the entire next day, which happened to be Valentine's Day.

When she went to her bank to cash a check that morning, she was immediately assaulted by the sight of bouquets of flowers on all the secretarys' and tellers' desks. An indoor rose garden.

In the past, such a sight had made her a bit sad. Everyone loved, everyone remembered. Happily Ever Afters on every desk, all over the world, from bosses to college interns. But on this particular Valentine's Day she did not feel such an affront. The potential lover on her computer—just a click away—buffered her usual despair. The teller gave her a smile and a little pink candy heart enclosed in a plastic wrapper with her money. The candy heart was stamped with the mauve words "Truly Yours."

She smiled back. She didn't need to feel excluded from Happily Ever Afters today, as a facsimile of them was waiting at home. Handy fix-it Max. His sentences.

His underground house. The Harley he would drive her around upon, someday, to see the Adirondack mountains.

Her sister Brianna called that night. "Hey, sis, happy Valentine's Day! Come over and have some pie; the girls and I made chocolate cream pie as a surprise for Peter. And I am making your favorite for dinner . . . shepherd's pie!"

"Oh, I think I'll stay in," Alana replied. Rather than head over to see her sister's family—the kids were really so cute and sweet and even fought over her, like she was a shiny, irresistible toy—she wanted to stay home and look again at Max's photographs and missives.

"C'mon!" Brianna said. "We haven't seen you in weeks. You're becoming a stranger!"

Which was true: Alana had stopped visiting them, or going anywhere much, come to think of it.

"Okay," she said. A drive would be good for her. And it would be nice to see how it felt to be *Alana in an almost couple with Max*, in the presence of her sister, who didn't mean to be cruel but always did manage to rub her happiness in Alana's face.

"Peter and the girls and I are thinking Aruba this year," she might call to report.

Or:

"You should see the naughty little thing Peter got me!"

Or:

"I think this weekend will be a stay-at-home-and-play-board-games family weekend."

Brianna rarely called to ask about how she was doing, or talk about the news or a book she was reading or a special story about just one of the girls. Or even the weather, and everybody talks about the weather. Somehow, everything she said always had a subtext: *I am the proud owner of a Happily Ever After family. (And you are not, alas. So sorry, dear sister.)*

Driving her car, Alana flipped on the radio. The deejay was playing songs that had been dedicated from one person to another. "This one goes out to Alyssa from her man, Ray," he said, followed by the poppy, happy Romantics tune "What I Like About You."

"And this next one is for Samantha, from a secret admirer." It was that Elvis song "Blue Velvet." How campy. She wondered if Samantha was listening and if she knew who this secret admirer was, and what the song meant to her.

But she, too, had a secret now. And while it still wasn't a real live man that she could cook breakfast for or walk on a beach with, per se, it was real, right? Her computer was real, for example, wasn't it? And the messages she received on it were real, actual words, from an actual somebody. Who happened to be very cute and, p.s., currently the builder of an actual underground house.

When she knocked on the door of her sister's house, Alana heard the stampede of little feet. "I got it!" "No, I do!"

A battle was breaking out. "I get first dibs on Auntie Alana."

Megan, the smallest of the three children, liked to brush Alana's hair and put multitudes of colorful barrettes in it, all over. There were many pictures documenting this: Alana at Hanukkah, with barrettes; at Easter (yes, they were Jewish but celebrated all holidays for the girls—they were an equal-opportunity holiday family), Alana with little duck barrettes all over. Halloween: Alana with black skeleton barrettes all over.

Megan greeted her, hair brush at the ready, her small hands immediately pulling her down to her level. "Hi hi hi, girls, hello hello!" Alana said, swaying over in Megan's oddly strong grip . . . then handing over her traditional gift of organic lollipops.

"Yay!"

"The green one is mine."

"I wanted the green one, you took it!"

"I got dibs on that one. I'm telling Mom!"

Another skirmish.

"Break it up, break it up," said Peter, policing through the tiny mob. "Hello, dearest sister-in-law," he said, hugging her. He always smelled of Old Spice and cookies, whatever the occasion, every day of the year. He was a handsome guy, this husband of her sister. In the past his good looks and affable, bright personality had often stung her with pin pricks of jealousy. But on this occasion, it was different. She felt not a whit of it. In the cage in her heart where jealousy had hummed and rattled was a warmth, the humming, spinning warm thing of potential Max pushing old jealousy out the door. It had unpacked its baggage of really good cycles and underground houses and moved right in.

"You look different somehow," Peter remarked.

"New shirt," Alana answered,

"No, you really do," said Brianna, entering the room with a masher in one hand and a bowl of potatoes in the other. She walked over and planted a kiss on Alana's cheek.

"Did you do something new to your hair?"

"No, but I have a feeling Megan has something new in mind for me." Megan jumped up and down beside her. "Just a few minutes, sweetie," Alana said. "Let me hang out with Mommy a bit first. Go and play." She walked into the kitchen, where a gigantic bouquet of roses on the island in the middle of the room nearly assaulted her. "Wow, feeling guilty about something, is he?" Alana laughed.

Brianna did not find this funny. She frowned. "Don't act so jealous."

"Oh, I'm not, really, they're gorgeous!"

On the counter was an open laptop with a recipe for shepherd's pie on the screen. Alana fought the urge to walk over to it and check her e-mail for a new message from Max.

"What's new?" she asked.

The kitchen actually was the new thing, a brand spanking renovation, and a Valentine's Day present to Brianna, with granite counters, a giant Cadillac of a stove, and a refrigerator that could chill the entire country of Paraguay. Alana had seen it as a work in progress, and a bit excessive, to be honest. The sort of gift one should get for a twentieth anniversary, or some really big celebration.

"I mean aside from all this," she said, gesturing around. "It looks amazing, by the way." Alana thought, despite all the newness of it, the sparkling showroom quality, it seemed slightly less cheery than usual. Since the remodel, Brianna had taken down all the little drawings and paintings the girls had done over the years. "I miss their art, though," she said.

"Oh, we'll get plenty more soon," Brianna said, "don't worry. We've got three little artists living here."

"Well, send some art my way when you get a surplus. My house is looking a bit dingy, it could use some cheering up. Smells good in here, Bree."

"It's the pie, shhh." She put her finger to her lips. "The secret pie."

Every year Brianna made Peter a "secret pie," and every year he played at surprise and shock and the girls exploded in giggles. This was the sort of thing Happily Ever After families did.

While Brianna stirred potatoes, Peter was out in the garage doing some manly garage thing. While on other occasions it had rankled a bit, all this busy happiness and happy business, on this day it did not. Alana actually felt happy to be there as well, a part of their buzzing world. She settled in the family room on the floor for her barrette session and colored with the older girls on the coffee table. Brianna put on some music in the kitchen. They were her family, too, she thought. Why had she never thought of it this way before?

Soon dinner was ready, and she snuck away from Megan's tiny fingers to wash her hands. There, on a desk in his office, she spied Peter's laptop, open and even on, casting its white glow out toward the window behind. Oh, how much she wanted to jump on it and just for a second look at Max on his bike again, with the wind in his hair and a new picture, too, Max and his dog, Ike, a hearty shepherd-Lab mix. "Ike says HI!" he wrote, in the caption.

She tiptoed in. Entering Peter's office was sort of verboten in the house. He was very private, the author of novels that, no matter what they were about, somehow always featured hunting and deer. He worked from home.

Feeling guilty, Alana closed the door quietly behind her and was about to sit down on the big Aeron chair in front of it when she peered ahead and then caught her breath, sucked it right back in, a vague sense of electric shock flying through her. She actually tingled from toes to fingertips.

On the screen was a woman, posed in the most uncompromising fashion. Spread-eagle. Her tongue hanging out of her mouth, in such a way that it struck Alana as slovenly, really ridiculous. It wasn't so much her nudity spread across the screen of her brother-in-law's computer, that wide-open beaver thing, that mortified her as it was that flicked tongue. It was a lower-class thing to do with one's tongue, a cartoon thing, something her sister Bree would never do, never even imagine doing. She felt the tongue actually violating her sister's home, insulting her family, the whole Happily Ever After of them on suddenly unsteady ground. Shaking herself, like a wet dog, as if she could somehow slough off the sense of shock, she slipped back out of the office. She wanted to get away from the brash, tongue-wagging bottle-blonde secret girl back to the acceptable secret chocolate pie of the kitchen, as fast as possible. God forbid Peter should see her in there.

"What is the matter with you, Alana?" her sister said. "You look like you saw a ghost."

Alana tried to smile, feebly. "I was just thinking about Mom and Dad," she said, trying to cover her lingering shock, the actual physical lightning bolt she had felt careening through her. Their parents had been dead for a few years; they went one right after the other, from a heart attack and a stroke (Dad, heart attack; Mom, stroke).

"You must have just seen the portrait I put of them in the den." Brianna smiled. "It's from our vacation, that time."

"Yes," said Alana. She walked out of the kitchen to take a deep breath of air and to look at it. There were the four of them, standing inside Carlsbad Caverns. Brianna and Alana holding hands. Their mother in a charcoal-colored dress with a matching sweater, wearing a sun hat, her dad in jeans and a button-down sweater. Alana walked back into the kitchen and stood beside her sister.

"Cool picture of us, right?"

"Remember how scared you were in the cave, when it was so dark?"

"Actual dark," said Brianna, quoting the guide. "Without a drop of light."

"Yes," Alana said. The vision of the woman and her tongue seemed like it was floating somewhere on the newly painted yellow wall above the refrigerator, a ghost, or an afterimage, imprinted on her eyelids, flashing.

She took the spoon from Brianna's hand. "Go play with the girls, it's your turn—I can finish here."

"Really, Ally? Okay! There is the recipe . . . on the computer. It's shepherd's pie, just add the potatoes on top and . . ."

"I can read! Really! Go!" She prodded her sister's arm with the wooden spoon.

Brianna smiled and scurried out. She was actually quite happy to have a minute with the girls. "Ask Megan to do your hair . . . get the new look—it's some kind of a punk thing . . . all the rage . . ."

Brianna laughed. Her laughter sounded so innocent and fragile, like a thing that could be smashed into pieces.

Alana spread the potatoes atop the pie and popped the concoction in the oven. Checked the temperature and time. She stirred frozen orange juice into a pitcher. She wiped the granite counter with a sponge. She felt odd, as if the photograph on Peter's computer had somehow infected her. She washed her hands.

Then she gave in to the urge. She looked around and then clicked into her e-mail on the kitchen laptop. Up popped a new message. From Max. She clicked it open. A virtual bouquet of rosebuds appeared. Clicked on, they bloomed. "For you, my new girl!" said a note that popped up at the end. His girl. She was Max's virtual girl. His potential Alana. And he was her potential Max.

Imaginary Max. Safe Max. Underground house Max. Nobody can hurt you if they are merely potential.

Just then Alana realized something; a fact settled in her heart like windswept soil. She realized she would keep Max just like this, as long as she could and possibly forever. Real Max could potentially lie, abuse, or use her, cheat, steal, behave meanly. He could break her heart, leave sticky piles of socks around . . . forget her birthday. So she would keep him right there on the screen, at arm's length, a click away, neither dismiss him nor invite him in closer. Max could live in her computer, under circuits and a motherboard and back inside the walls of her house, and in the electricity of the greater world, buzzing around in an infinitely coded fashion.

She thought of the picture at her sister's house. The photograph was of the four of them, inside Carlsbad Caverns, with the cave all around them. Stalactites reaching down, like longing arms of fire. They were actually underground. And if she remembered correctly, for that brief time, that snapshot of a moment, they were happy.

The Opposite of Love

Rita's mother called to congratulate her on the new position, tenure track (!) at the branch college. It was a big deal; there had been only a handful of positions available that spring in the entire country. After the downturn, most state funds dried up. Most college searches were canceled entirely. The only reason hers wasn't canceled was that the economic collapse had shut down almost all job hiring as well, so there was a tsunami of student applications to state schools. Since there was nothing else to do, people were going back to school. This made for a particularly bland sort of student, prone to writing papers on their favorite television episodes.

"I hope this makes you happy," her mother had said when she called Rita. She had always felt her daughter was a sourpuss, a person unable to see the glass half full. She had even taken to calling her "glass-half-empty girl." "How is glass-half-empty girl today?" she might ask, when Rita called. Her sister, Martha, a life coach in Topanga Canyon, was perpetually cheery, a fact her mother never missed an opportunity to point out.

What did it even mean to be happy? Rita thought. She knew she was lucky, certainly, to be hired at such a time. And she, without even a PhD to her name. It was some sort of rare academic coup. She was like the Urania moth of professors. The Urania was so rare everyone thought it had become extinct until it was photographed by an unknowing tourist on a hike in the Peruvian rain forest. She'd read about it in *National Geographic* at her doctor's office.

But, as so often happens, her good news came with bad. While getting the job had constituted a stroke of good luck, her being at the doctor's was a stroke of bad luck.

She'd gotten breast cancer and the job simultaneously. She had found a job at a time when there were no jobs, and breast cancer at the same time it seemed everyone was getting breast cancer. It was like the disease of the month. A woman next door to her mother, her sister's best friend, two people who worked at her dry cleaner's, and even one woman's husband had it. The woman was the receptionist at the YMCA where Rita worked out. "We couldn't believe it; he doesn't even have breasts the way some men do, those man-boobs," she exclaimed. "He doesn't have those!"

Many famous people were getting it, too. This made everybody feel a little better—that money and fame were no firewall. It increased its wattage as the disease du jour. They, of course, had made going bald from the chemo look a little chic and even a little beautiful when they went on *Ellen* and *Oprah* and talked about how they were getting through it with the help of their fans and frequent trips to Bali to consult native healers.

In an even crazier trick of fate, Rita had found her lump the same day she got the letter about the job. She told everyone about the job, but told nobody about the lump, which felt nothing like a lump at all. A *lump* was a large and nebulous thing. What was inside her felt exactly as if someone had buried a pea—a secret pea, like the one the princess could feel under all those mattresses—only her pea was right under her nipple. The problem, as she understood it from the doctors she had spoken with so far, was that this pea might sprout and begin to grow, filling her body with pea plants, leafy and muscular, curling their little tendrils all around her heart, her organs, the twin engines of her lungs, filling her with peas, everywhere, until she was more pea than she was Rita. A walking invisible vegetable garden.

Had it not been for that little novel she had written two summers ago (accidentally, almost—while helping her mother clean out the attic, she had found all those old journals of her great-grandmother—it practically wrote itself), she would have never gotten the job. As for the breast cancer, it was mysterious to her. *Who had planted that first pea there?* she wondered. Was it something she ate? Something she breathed in? Something she drank that contained the smallest-ever particles of cancer pea?

"Spectacular," *The New Yorker* had raved, about her book. "Absolutely," said the oncologist, who had done the final and definitive test. "You're hired," said the dean of Arts and Science, at the branch college. And, with those words, her literary, academic career and her new identity as a cancer patient were born. Funny, she thought, how a teensy novel and some teensy words and a teensy pea of cancer could change your life so much, in ways both good and bad.

"Good morning, class," she said, the first day she began teaching. She handed out the syllabus she had carefully put together. It had the reading list and the assignments that would be due, one by one, in a list down the left-hand side. One student put his head down on his desk after glancing over it and made an audible sigh, as if it was so much work he had already grown tired. Another asked: "Are *all* these books in the bookstore already?"

"Yes," said Rita. "They are all in." What did they think, these college students, that they would not even be reading any books in an English class?

The branch college was a small one in a very small town in a far-flung place, almost at the Canadian border. A place she had begun to call "the edge of the known world." She thought she was like the Magellan of assistant professors, sent to seek out and colonize young minds with interesting thoughts here in the hinterlands—while simultaneously, inside her, a small colony of its own had taken hold. One she must stamp out with the help of the oncology department at the hospital in the new town.

"I'm happy, I'm happy already," she had replied to her mother. It would be far too upsetting to tell her about the breast cancer. Besides, she thought if she could just keep it a secret, it would hardly exist, this little pea starting its life inside her. If she told her mother, soon everyone would know and it would give that little pea more legitimacy, its own cheering squad almost. In front of her class she wondered if anyone could see it, this illness beginning its life. Did it show itself to certain people, perhaps? Or make her seem vulnerable?

"We will read a book every two weeks. We will discuss them in class and then you will write two-page papers on each of them," she said. "There will be a final." She felt like adding, *Can you handle that?*

After teaching she would head to the YMCA and sit for a long time in the steam room. She had the feeling it was cleansing her somehow, inside and out. Sweating out bad molecules, bad thoughts. Bad stuff (mood leftover from whiny students, evil cancer stress vibes) out. Good stuff (heat, water) in.

Happy, schmappy, she thought, in the steam room. You could certainly not be happy when you had cancer, could you? The word itself had a sort of silly sound to it even. Happy. Like the name of a clown or the punch line to a joke in a children's book. What do you get if you mix sappy with a sneeze? Ha—ha—ha—happiness. What do you call a man who likes to pee? Happy. Get it, TWO "p"s? Bad jokes from the kindergarten set.

Rita had always thought happiness was overrated, anyway, the emotion for the masses. Something advertised daily on national television. This new car, or that vacation or this food or that medication . . . voilà! Happiness!

She was much more interested in other human sentiments. She particularly cultivated irony, sarcasm, sardonicness (was there a "ness" on the end? She would have to look that up), and even a freckle or so of out-and-out despair. Despair, after all, was appropriate when you lived on a planet on the brink of collapse in a society that insisted on declaring war every ten minutes on places so far away most of her students had never even heard of them, and with a disease that could begin to sprout and grow inside you at any given moment. Happiness was the drug they fed you to keep you from noticing all this.

For this reason she was pleased when she found out she would be teaching a course called "Irony in Western Literature" in the spring at the college, rather than English 102, which she had been assigned to teach on her arrival. She wasn't sure exactly what they would read yet, or what she would teach, but she simply loved the sound of the course, the way you might look forward to a large unsweetened beverage on a hot day. The right sort of drink, one that would not give you cavities or cancer or add a spare tire around your waist. An irony cocktail.

Late at night, when she got home from the new college in the new town, she went online to a cancer "discussion forum" and shared her feelings about the diagnosis with people as far away as Hong Kong and Cape Town and Iowa City. There was even a man on a boat somewhere off the coast of Newfoundland in the cancer discussion forum.

"The funny thing is, I just don't feel that different," the man said. His name was Henrik. He was a lifelong fisherman.

"I do," said Rita. "I feel like I have been invaded by an alien."

"But that is how you feel in your mind, do you feel any different in your body?"

"Not yet," she said, "but they start the radiation next month." That was how it worked. First the surgery, then chemo and radiation.

"Yeah, I hear that kicks your ass."

It was hard to imagine anything kicking Henrik's ass. He had faced storms at sea and several bouts of pneumonia, and had lost a finger once in a machine that cleaned fish. He was a tough guy.

Her surgery was quick and easy enough, the lumpectomy. It was actually an outpatient procedure. She had it on a Friday and was back at work on Monday. Her breast didn't even feel any different. She had been afraid to feel for the pea, that it might still be there.

Days, Rita taught *Hamlet* and *Pride and Prejudice* and geared up to teach *Things Fall Apart* and *The Good Earth*. Nights, she went online to talk to Henrik and a woman named Anna Lin, who taught English in Japan. After four weeks, she began radiation and chemo.

It may have been her imagination, but Rita began to sense something happening between Henrik and Anna Lin, a kind of attraction, blossoming. While she would talk about her classes and the treatment, her nausea, the way she would vomit in secret at a bathroom in the janitor's office at the college, how she hid her illness like a crime she was committing, Anna Lin and Henrik would talk about their favorite movies, the best foods to eat after chemo.

They would share articles they found online about people who had survived the disease and done amazing things. Henrik's favorite book was Lance Armstrong's *It's Not About the Bike*. Rita secretly suspected the athlete's cancer could have been caused by the steroids he used over the course of his career as a bike racer, but she didn't say anything. Cancer patients, on the whole, try to avoid the topic of blame.

In mid-November, when she was handing back some essays to her 102 class, a student raised his hand. His name was Bruno, he was on the ice hockey team, and he had a head of thick, curly black hair. Rita had recently become aware of hair and how much or little people had of it, since hers had begun to come out in clumps when she combed it, the way you might pull up flowers, accidentally when you are weeding. She had purchased some extensions she clipped onto her remaining hair that were actually kind of attractive, she thought. She might even look better than she ever looked. Cancer was honing her features, refining them. Or chemo was. In any case she thought she looked more real somehow.

"How do you think we are supposed to keep up with all this reading?" Bruno asked. "We've got games this week and next."

Are you joking? she thought. It was such a cliché, the college athlete complaining about the actual academic work.

"Coach says you are giving us too much; he is going to report it."

Rita could see some of the other students nodding.

"Okay, poll: How many of you think this class has been too much work? We have a total of five books and five short essays in here," she said. "One final. Is that really too much?"

A slight girl with a pierced nose raised her hand. "It is just the reading. It's a lot. Some of these books are long, and kinda hard to read."

"Okay, poll: Does everyone feel like that?"

The class nodded in unison. "Okay, duly noted," Rita said. "I'll get back to you on this."

After class she went to the janitor's closet bathroom and threw up.

She was certain she had read much more than she was assigning in her own college 102 class. She was certain she had had to write more essays and take more tests, too. Nevertheless, she decided to lighten the load. "You have to choose your battles," she told her mother, on the phone, explaining the decision.

"That you do," her mother said. She still hadn't told her about the cancer.

That night, she went online and saw that Henrik and Anna Lin had created their own private chat room. She could see it but not enter; they had it "locked." There were four other cancer forums she could go to, but somehow none of them appealed to her. She felt sort of left out of the discussion with Henrik and Anna Lin. She had begun to think of them as her secret cancer family. They were in there talking for over two hours, without her. Then, at about eleven, just as she was turning off her computer and about to go to sleep, she got an IM from Anna Lin.

"Rita—you still up?"

"Yeah, planning my classes for the week. Gotta scale back, apparently I assigned too much work!"

"Guess what?!"

"What?"

"Henrik is coming to visit me! He is coming to Japan!"

"Are you joking?"

"No, he is coming this weekend!"

"But what about his chemo?"

"He just finished it up. And he says he feels okay. He said I make him feel better."

"Wow."

"I know, double wow, right?"

"Right!"

Anna hung up and Rita just sat there, feeling surprised and a little jealous. It wasn't that she wanted to be Henrik's best cancer buddy. She just didn't want to be nobody's cancer buddy.

The weekend went by and Rita bought apples and made applesauce, which she had heard was good for nausea. She graded papers and picked which book to take off the reading list. All the books were classics, and she didn't like the feeling she was snubbing one. But it had to be. She was choosing her battles. On Monday she told her class. "Okay, I want you to know I am hearing you. And I am taking *The Good Earth* off the list for this class. It makes me a little sad because it is a truly great book, a book of triumph over adversity, and hope and love, and I hope you all read it someday, like over the holiday . . ." She heard a snicker. "But for now we will omit it."

The class broke out in applause. It was the biggest rise she had gotten from them since she began teaching. That afternoon a clump of hair fell out that was so big it could no longer be hidden by the extensions. She was going to have to get a wig.

Rita thought about it. Why was it that rock stars and actresses could go bald and everyone loved them more for it, but she felt it would make her vulnerable at work? She was a new hire, and here she was already sick. And with the big C. She felt she had to *hide* it. But hiding it was getting harder and harder.

Then, it happened: She ran into the department secretary at the hospital as she was coming out of the place where she got her chemo, a large bank of chairs hooked up to the drip-drip-dripping bags of the medication that eradicated the cancer, tethered to a mysterious fluid, liquid poison, meant to all but kill you, knocking out the little pea plants on the way.

They would all sit there like that, some people reading magazines, others listening to their iPods, every now and then taking a swig of a drink. Nobody spoke. It reminded Rita of the banks of women sitting under the dryers at the beauty parlor when she'd gone with her mother as a child. Each one wrapped in a plastic mechanism, separate, eyes glued to a magazine, or the rare book. All in a row.

"Hello, Dr. Friedman," said the secretary. "How are you? I mean, are you . . . sick?"

"Hi, Lucy," said Rita, pausing. Right over her head was the bold "Chemotherapy Unit" sign. "Yes, I am. I have breast cancer."

"Oh, so do I!" said the secretary, sort of excitedly. It was like a big club, this thing, breast cancer, inducting new members daily. "Maybe we can go on the walk together."

"The walk?"

"The breast cancer awareness walk. You missed this one; we have one every October, downtown."

"Of course," said Rita. "We'll have to."

The next day, in her mail cubby in the department, she found a soft pink ribbon pin. *Pink is the color of little girls' bedrooms, of cotton candy and breast cancer,* Rita thought. *Now I will have to wear pink clothes and go on walks and be a rah-rah cancer cheerleader.* It was something her sister—the life coach—would have been so much better at. Her sister was better at most things, and she would have been better at being sick as well, the whole gestalt of it. Rita, on the other hand, just wanted to chat online again with Anna Lin and Henrik, grab some midnight solace, their deeply sardonic yammer. But they had disappeared from her computer screen, enjoined in their own cancer support group of two, somewhere in Japan.

Her students, Rita thought, were looking at her differently. What was it? They seemed kinder, gentler, a whole new breed of student, as if someone had been washing them with fabric softener. "Dr. Friedman," said one, after class, "I read *The Good Earth*. I loved it. I know we didn't have to, but it was on my shelf and I . . ." It was the girl named Amanda, who had big cornflower-blue eyes and short hair, who wore interesting yet bizarrely violent-looking earrings.

"You did? I am so glad. What did you like about it?"

"I liked how Wang Lung and his wife were so poor but happy and then how they became wealthy and unhappy. And how she, well, didn't she get . . . breast cancer, his wife?" The girl looked straight into Rita's eyes.

"You never know for certain, but yes, that is indicated."

"My mother has it," the girl said. "Breast cancer."

"Oh," said Rita, "I am so sorry."

She felt the girl waiting, standing there, as if Rita would say something else. *Now I am supposed to do it, out this thing, this illness, tell the world. This is the moment.* She felt certain that the department secretary must have told this girl, and maybe everyone. But she couldn't. She couldn't say anything. No word would form in her mouth. She felt it had to be a silent thing. Something only Henrik and Anna Lin and others in the cancer chats could know about. Nobody in her walking, driving, teaching, or family life.

That night she got an e-mail from Anna Lin. "Rita!" it said. "I am engaged to Henrik! I had to tell you, you are the only one who might understand. We fell in love, it is so amazing, and strange and . . . beautiful even, two sickos like us, all kissy face and sweetie-pied out."

Rita wrote back: "I am so happy for you, Anna, and for Henrik. Please tell him. Mazel tov, as we say in my tribe."

The next day she got two e-mails. The first was from Anna Lin. "Thank you," it said.

The second was from her mother. "You might have told me, Rita, that you are sick! You might have told your own MOTHER. But I guess we really aren't that close. I would have wished for you to be able to come to me."

Like your sister, Rita thought, filling in the rest of the sentence. The department secretary knew somebody who was a friend of somebody who was a friend of someone else, so that somehow through the web that becomes a vine that is Facebook, her mother had read the news. She'd been outed. She had breast cancer. And she felt truly sick now, from the chemo, and weak, and all her hair was gone. Even her eyebrows. She had begun wearing a bad wig, like an orthodox woman.

Her mother was angry! It actually was as if Rita had joined some elite club and left her out. Her mother would have liked to have gone on cancer awareness walks and worn a pink pin and embraced this disease for her. Made some happy times of it. Some memories! She could have made an album with her friends in their scrapbooking club. Helping Rita get through breast cancer! She felt it was her RIGHT as a mom. And Rita had denied her this, selfish as she was. She had hoarded her cancer and kept it to herself. A secret treasure chest of cells, multiplying within her. A whole booty of special cells, twirling and whirling, jitterbugging and spiraling through her.

In the spring, Rita began teaching the class on irony but without the initial zeal she had felt for it. She stood before her class, feeble and thin, wearing the pink pin and her wig, trying hard to be the soldier in the army of the stricken everyone seemed to want her to be. She passed around a handout on all the different flavors of irony: Socratic, dramatic, verbal, literary, situational. "Let's talk about irony," she said. "What does this word mean to you?"

"The use of words to convey a meaning that is the opposite of its literal meaning," said a student in the front row, who had obviously been boning up on it, in preparation for the first day. She looked over at the woman. It was Amanda, she of the blue eyes, the virulent earrings, the boyish-cut hair.

"Hello, Amanda! Nice to see you in here. Can you give an example?"

"Yes," said the girl. "An infatuated boy leaves a girl flowers to wish her luck during her upcoming recital. Her protective father becomes upset that she's getting flowers from boys and as a result of the argument over the good-luck flowers, she is late and misses the recital . . ."

"Very good, anything else you can think of?"

The class was silent. Minds spinning, trying to think of examples.

"A gourmet cook eating Chicken McNuggets?" asked one kid.

"Yes!"

"A swimming instructor who drowns?"

"Yes!"

Then Amanda raised her hand. "Can you give us an example, Professor Friedman?"

Rita hadn't been prepared for it. In fact, she was feeling unprepared for just about everything these days. "Well, I heard about a pop star who got malaria while filming a malaria awareness commercial. But wait, I have a better example." Rita walked to the front of the desk and leaned against it, looking out at the sea of faces. They looked at her with anticipation. They were hungry for the other example of irony.

"A woman writer gets her dream job as a professor, teaching about irony in literature, but that same day she gets a phone call. 'You have breast cancer,' she is told. 'It is stage two.'"

The class was silent, waiting for the ironic part.

"What is ironic about that?" one student finally asked. "Exactly?"

"Well, she has her dream come true in life, but she is going to die."

Suddenly the class seemed to see her, her frailty, her skeletal frame. Her bad wig. Her whole demeanor. And the pink pin on top, like a rose made of frosting on a cake. She was their dying professor of irony.

"I am so sorry," Amanda said. "I thought you were doing better."

In fact, she was. She had completed the treatment and was waiting for the results of tests; "It all looked very good," her oncologist had told her. But late the previous night she had opened a single e-mail, sent to her inbox from a real person, in the sea of spam hawking everything from Ab Magic to home business opportunities to a letter from a sheik who said he owed her two million dollars. The lone e-mail was from Henrik. She braced herself for the onslaught of happiness news. Wedding pictures, perhaps an invitation. Their online love had taken and bloomed. They would survive cancer together, each one a raft of hope for the other.

"This is about Anna Lin," Henrik wrote. "She got pneumonia . . . double pneumonia actually, it was all very fast and she was just too weak . . . She didn't respond well to any treatment. She will be buried in her family's plot in Worcester, Mass., next week. I thought you should know. Henrik."

Rita blinked back a veneer of tears as she scrolled through the message several times. There was nothing ironic in it. Nothing at all. It was just shocking, and sad.

She had been so jealous of them, of their bond. Rita just sat there and stared at the computer screen for a long time, as if looking at it could somehow rearrange the message, bring Anna back to life. Or make it not so, some dream of an e-mail.

"What is ironic about that," Rita told her inquiring student, "is that the professor thought she had just won the lottery of life, getting this amazing job teaching you all. But in fact she was facing her own death. The lottery doled out a life and a death sentence at the same time."

The class was silent. Nobody spoke. Everyone felt sad, but they were also unsure if this was a good example of irony. Was it? The minutes ticked away and Rita didn't speak either. One by one the students shuffled out of the room.

Long before this happened, years before, Rita's boyfriend Alex, the love of her life, had broken up with her. It had taken her by surprise. She had thought they were happy. Or at least okay. There had been no fight, no incident precipitating the breakup. Just one day he came over and said, "I think we are over."

How could he leave? Was he angry at her? Had she hurt him in some way she did not know? Didn't he love her? Did he hate her? He had taken her hand and looked right into her face. "Rita, the opposite of love isn't hate."

"What?" she asked.

"I realized that, in our relationship."

"What is it then, the opposite of love?"

"It's indifference," he said. "Just feeling nothing."

She often thought about that, the feeling of nothing. A blank space, a caesura, a hole-punch in the heart.

At Anna Lin's funeral, Rita finally met Henrik. To her surprise he was a much older man than she thought, a man with a limp, who leaned heavily into a carved wooden cane. He wore ill-fitting clothes and spoke with a stutter that was so severe as to make him almost incomprehensible.

"I lo, lo, love, loved her," he said. "I, I, I, didididd." He was weeping.

"I know," said Rita, who had driven eight hours, shakily, to make the funeral. She wrapped her thin arms around him and felt, for the first time, as if this cancer had brought her closer to someone in the world. "You cared so much. She knew that."

He bowed his head and it touched the top of her head. Their two foreheads pressed together hard, actually adhering a little through some combination of sweat and the elastic properties of skin and sadness. They were bent into a sort of triangle of grief. Between them there was a feeling she could not name. But it seemed to her then that, if such a thing could be, it was the very most opposite thing in the world from irony. The opposite of love. The opposite of happiness. The opposite of opposite. The opposite of all known and yet-to-be-known things.

Boat Man

Allison had a special sponge for cleaning the inside of glasses, thin with a scrubby green tip, perfect for removing the goo from the O.J. glass, sludge from old coffee mugs, whatever that stuff was in the bottom of her father's Ensure.

She gave him a cup full of that crap twice a day. It came in cans and was touted as the ultimate nutrition. But when she read the ingredients it sounded more like a chemistry experiment. *This is what they feed us*, she thought, *at the end, when we have no choice.* Whenever she gave it to him he winced. Her father, Joe, had been a sous-chef at a five-star French restaurant. She had been serving him the stuff for four years. *That is 365 times four*, she thought, doing the math, *minus one day for leap year.* That made 1,459 days of a drink that was an insult to his every taste bud. She felt a surge of guilt flood her veins like some distant cousin of adrenaline, pumped out of a special guilt gland, secreted away in the corner of her heart. Her guilt gland was very active.

Allison also had sponges for the kitchen counter. Smooth but tough, to get off the schmutz without scratching the Formica. She had a really intense sponge for stuff burned onto the bottoms of casseroles. And, of course, she had steel wool. Steel wool, wool of steel, harvested from the flock of steel sheep that grazed on Iron Mountain, she thought. It worked for the worst-case scenarios. Crusted meat loaf that will not release from the pan; that grainy brown material that comes about if you leave the cereal bowl sitting for an afternoon.

Yes, Allison had a plethora of cleaning tools, and it actually made her feel happy to have options when she was doing dishes. She would look into her cabinet and there they were, organized in neat bins, according to the difficulty of the task. Laugh if you want, but it worked for her. And, by the way, if you ever find yourself in a life that revolves completely around taking care of someone else, wiping the drool off his chin, the poop off his butt, because his brain decided to take a long hike and his body said "I think I'll just stay here behind . . . ," well, we will remember not to laugh at you for your organizational schemes.

Just as Allison had her sponge-filing system, she had developed a love strategy. She had Doctorlove.com for highbrow online dating; Letsgethooked.com for serious dating; Flirtypants.com for flirting, and Yummybaby.com for when she felt like slumming it. She had paid a small fee to belong to each of these communities, and within each of them she felt comfortable. She had a system. "A girl needs a system," she liked to quip, if anyone asked why so many, or why at all, about anything.

"Like, do you ever, like, meet anyone in there you, like, think is for real?" asked Babette, her best friend forever, or her BFF, as she liked to say. The two had known each other since kindergarten.

Even though she was pushing fifty, Allison liked to use the online vernacular of those thirty-five years younger than she. It made her feel relevant. "IDK," she wrote back, "jury is still out."

And the jury was definitely out, she thought. For who in his right mind would want a woman saddled with an eighty-eight-year-old father who could not feed himself? A man so divorced from his former self that he no longer even remembered his own name? "That would be one hell of an online man," said Babette.

"Yeah, thanks for that insight there," Allison said.

Then, two weeks before her fifty-first birthday, it seemed just such a man appeared.

"Yo hey," he wrote in an instant message. "Cool old white dude seeks happening mate!"

"Yeah hi," she wrote back. "Very happening white chick seeks cool old dude."

And so their banter began. They chatted this a way and that a way, they talked yoga and pie crust, sunsets and anime. They talked books (he was partial to Hemingway; she to Joyce Carol Oates). They talked poetry (he was a Billy Collins guy; she was an Anne Sexton gal). They talked music (Nirvana, him; Tori Amos, her) and art (Picasso, him; Judy Chicago, her). Film (*Seven Samurai*, him; *Harold and Maude*, her).

"Well, don't we just define the gender wars?" she wrote.

"That we do," he wrote back.

They each chuckled before their screens. Chuckled into a nothingness that was a somethingness that was the oblique landscape where they courted. A tangle of wires and laser signals, flipping through a cyberscape where no human foot could tread.

Their late-night texting habit would morph into conversations that would get so hot sometimes the phone burned her. (It actually did, because she had it on for so long and held it to her ear so tightly as she lay on the couch chatting. Her ear would turn cherry red . . . Research has revealed that this cell phone burn syndrome could prove devastating to brain tissue, possibly even cause deterioration and disease . . . something that a girl caring for an old man with dementia certainly worries over.)

But Allison was fifty and her brain still seemed fine. Her thumbs, on the other hand, were not as agile and fast as younger people's when it came to texting, but her mouth worked okay, so when they had those occasional phone calls in between marathon texting and e-mailing sessions, she learned a great deal about this man, whose name was Chuck. Including what seemed to her oddest of all the things she learned about him: Chuck lived, apparently, on a boat.

"Yeah? A boat?" she had asked.

"Twenty-five footer, a sloop," he wrote. "Call her *Tequila*. Or *Tila Tequila*. Depending on my mood."

"Like the drink, or the celebrity?"

"Just like that," he said, not answering.

He'd previously had a twenty-two-foot sloop named *Jenny*, this boaty man, but the *Tequila* was his baby. He had a life on the *Tequila*. A life at sea, or in harbor or at dock. Allison began to learn all about it, this existence. She heard about all the tasks involved, daily, in boat residence. Further, the problems that could come up. Like, say, leaks.

And what she did not learn about from their exchange, she learned of through his pictures. He sent her cell phone pictures of the boat that seemed purposely designed to give her very little bites of information. The boat was red. It had some scratches. The water was like a mirror reflecting the moon. There were frequent bird visitors.

When it stormed she found she was worried about this man Chuck on his boat. A man she had not once met. But Chuck told her not to bother worrying. In the winter he lived in the terrarium created by a taut coat of plastic shrink-wrap. He was like a hothouse plant in there, he said. "It is actually quite toasty," he insisted.

For his birthday, Allison made him curtains for the boat, tequila-themed. With bottles labeled "Mescal." She found the material online. She sent them by FedEx to the harbor address.

He, in turn, sent her groceries. They would come next-day air. Specialty foods she would never buy. Pumpkin butter and almond butter and cashew butter and goat cheese encased in tough herbed rinds; canned hominy. And soups, such soups, fresh dill and tomato bisque; things from Trader Joe's, where he apparently ran a credit line, this boat man, Chuck.

They told each other about their hobbies. Hers was kayaking across the pond near where she lived to the other side, where she was involved in an elaborate earth-work project. She would balance large stones atop other stones and make cairns. She would name them.

His was sailing in little regattas, going out to sea and coming back. Cleaning and rebuilding parts of the *Tequila* (a boat that *was* a girl, apparently, as he referred to it as "she"), and, for some time, replacing her windows. Making her "tight," as he said.

Chuck also liked yoga. He would do it on the deck of the *Tequila*. "One of the greatest myths of our time is that yoga must be done in a class," he wrote to Allison. After each e-mail he sent her, he wrote, "Namaste." A yoga salutation, she learned. She hadn't done much yoga, but she did like the fact that it came with its own lingo. "I spent the morning in Child's Pose," he would write. She looked it up: Child's Pose. And imagined him rocking on the *Tequila*, folded up on his knees like a seabird, nesting.

Oh, and one other little hobby, or favorite activity, this Chuck had: He liked to go to the little pub near the harbor. He went there almost every night. Maybe that explained the mornings spent in Child's Pose, she thought. Hangover?

Allison told her friends and family very little about Chuck. "He lives on a boat," she told her friend Elisa.

"And that's not weird?" Elisa replied. But then Elisa lived in a McMansion in Norwalk. She would think most things weird.

She told her sister, Anika, "He does a lot of yoga."

"And you like that . . . why?"

"I don't know, he seems nice," she said.

"Well, namaste to that," Anika joked.

"Right," she said.

And to her very best friend Babette, she wrote, "He sends me food."

"Why?" Babette asked.

"I think he is just being nice. It is very nice food."

"Well, food is good . . . ," Babette said.

The problem for Allison was not the yoga or the boat or the food but that this cool dude named Chuck was in the wrong category. She was very clear about her categories; she took them oh-so-seriously. And Chuck had not been in the serious dating category. She had met him on Yummybaby.com, not Letsgethooked.com, which she realized made her hesitate with him. Perhaps it was why she never suggested meeting. His boat was docked about an hour from where Allison lived, yet neither one had suggested a rendezvous. It had been almost six months.

She had a lot to do taking care of her father. Doctor's appointments, outings for fresh air, cleaning-up activities. She was busy. Not a lot of free time for boating. Or dating. Or dating on a boat. Or boating on a date. However you wanted to look at it.

"Mmm," said her father as she tipped his glass of Ensure to his mouth.

"Yes, mmm, Daddy, drink up."

He spat.

It was one of those unglamorous moments that characterized her life. The sort that make you want to hide from rather than meet people. So she continued her flirtation in the abstract: land woman, wiping old man up, and boat man, sailing the high seas.

Suddenly a car drove up. *Is it him?* she wondered. She was gardening again, her father parked in the shade. Out emerged a man in a brown uniform. "Truck broke down," he said. It was not the boat man but the UPS guy. He handed her a clipboard to sign. Then he handed her a box.

They had begun to send frequent packages, almost every other day, with photographs. She sent him a compass; he sent her groceries. She sent him a pair of warm socks. He sent more groceries. Chocolate-covered raisins. Mango jam. Whole-wheat pita bread. Macadamia nuts. She sent him a nice fountain pen. He sent pumpkin seeds. Rice cakes. Protein powder.

She took the package inside and went out to get her father. He watched her open the box. She fed him a small piece of chocolate and he smiled. "Mphgatagata-ahwaah," he said.

"Exactly my thoughts," she replied.

"Does he think I am poor?" she asked her friend Elin, on the phone that night.

"He thinks you are hungry," she replied.

"Maybe he is fattening you up," said Noa, the visiting nurse who helped her with her father once a week, taking his blood pressure. Checking his weight. Cleaning him up nicely.

"Like the witch was fattening Hansel?" asked Allison.

"Or like the crazy guy in *Silence of the Lambs*."

"Thanks for that image," Allison said.

"You started it," she laughed.

They sent each other more pictures they took with their cell phones. Allison sent him one of her kayak.

Chuck sent a picture of his left eye. She sent a picture of her oars; he sent a picture of his jaw. She sent pictures of her rock sculptures. He sent an ear. She began putting together the puzzle of him. But the jaw picture was too big for the eye picture and the ear was much, much too big. When she had assembled most of his face, he looked like a monster. Or a piece of art by David Hockney. Neither was particularly romantic. But taken apart the pictures were very appealing. It was a nice jaw. And a nice left eye, she thought. The ear was a perfectly acceptable-looking ear.

Around this time her father became ill and had to go into the hospital. His lungs, said the doctor, were "filling up."

"Filling up?" she asked.

"Yes," said the doctor.

"Is that bad?"

"Well, it isn't good."

"I mean is it normal?"

"It isn't abnormal."

In this way they spoke in circles. She noticed that most of her conversations with the doctor were like that, never getting anywhere in particular, just round and round.

But her conversations with Chuck were like arrows; they pierced to the heart of things. "I balanced a big rock on a bigger rock today, and the way it worked out there was a little window at the bottom you could peer through."

"And see the sun on the water," said Chuck.

"Yes."

"And the shore and houses," he said.

"Yes."

"You could frame things with the little window in the rocks."

"Exactly," she said.

When she told him her father was sick, that his lungs were filling up, Chuck said simply: "That is the way many old people die."

"It is?" she asked. It felt like he had stuck a vacuum hose down her throat and stopped her own lungs. She felt choked.

"Yes," he said.

The honesty sucked all the air out of her, but somehow it was also refreshing. It was a physical oxymoron. She called the doctor. "I hear this is how many old people die, their lungs filling up. Is that so?"

"It isn't a fiction," the doctor said.

"And when were you planning on telling me this?"

"I wasn't hiding anything."

Then the doctor was silent. His silence annoyed her but it also seemed to be indicative of something. He was not going to tell her things that might be uncomfortable. Or he would tell her just enough to not be lying. That night she called Chuck. "My dad is on a ventilator," she said.

"He is dying," said Chuck.

"Are you sure?" she asked.

"It is very likely," he said.

She swooned, actually felt her knees weaken. But she also felt her heart puff up, with something she thought might be love, for Chuck, the man on the boat, the only honest person in her life.

She sat next to her father the entire following week in the hospital. She held his hand and sang to him. She sang "New York, New York" and "Sunrise, Sunset" from *Fiddler on the Roof*, a song that had once made him tear up. She sang to him:

> *Summertime,*
> *And the livin' is easy*
> *Fish are jumpin'*
> *And the cotton is high.*

She had a beautiful voice. When she sang *Once I built a railroad, made it run, made it race against time . . .* she felt it. Her father squeezed her hand. "Daddy," she said, and she leaned over to kiss his cheek. He smiled.

By morning he was gone.

Allison took a break from Chuck for a few weeks. She was sitting shiva in her house. She had to write to everyone they knew, take care of the business that comes when a person who has lived a long time dies. "Closing up shop," her aunt Simcha called it.

Allison dropped off the wheelchair, the plastic device that made the toilet higher, the rails for the bed, at

Goodwill. When she drove back home there was a truck in front of her house. She thought it might be the UPS man again. "Is the UPS truck still broke down?" she asked the man sitting in the truck.

"What?" said the man.

"Your truck."

"Yes, it's mine. Wait—what do you mean?"

She recognized the voice. It was him. Chuck. The man on the boat. "Chuck?" she asked.

The man who was Chuck hopped out of the vehicle. He did not look like the boat man that she had had in her imagination. He did not look like the photographs from the cell phone. But if she looked at each part of him she recognized them. The eye, the jaw, the ear. But he was very, very small. Allison tried not to gape. He was . . . what was the word? Not a dwarf, because they had those largish heads and that particular shape to their faces. What was the word?

She remembered the time when she was about five and there had been a very small woman in the grocery store, in front of them in the line. "Look, Mama, an elf!" she had whispered.

Her mother had smiled. "There are no such things as elves," she said. "She is . . ."

"Allison?"

"Chuck!" she said.

Midget. That was the word. Or, in the politically correct vernacular of the moment, *little person.* He was very, very small and yet his nose was big, with veins on it, *from the alcohol,* she thought. *The bar by his sloop, the* Tequila.

"Well, come on in," she said, opening her front door. Inside were more boxes, her father's clothes; she was giving them all away. And boxes and boxes of Ensure. She had arranged to drive it to a nursing home one town over.

Chuck looked at the boxes of Ensure. "Terrible stuff," he said. "Poison, really."

"Yes, my father hated it."

"I brought you some . . ."

"Let me guess . . . groceries?" she asked, smiling.

"Yes," he said.

In the back of his truck were bags and bags of food. Boxes of bottled water. Exotic juices. Cheese from far, far away. Distant Nordic countries famed for their cheese. Wine from Brazil. *Who ever heard of Brazilian wine?* she thought. Seeds, nuts, dried fruit. Dried apple rings made into chips. *Apple chips! Who ever heard of apple chips?* It was more than she could eat in a year. A lifetime maybe.

And flowers. At least twenty huge sunflowers, with long, thick, fuzzy green stalks with fuzzy leaves. *The tallest flowers*, she thought as Chuck carried them inside, and that seemed to her like something that mattered.

"Thank you, Chuck," she said. Allison looked at him and he looked back, with the big sad eyes of the cell phone pictures. He glanced across the pond to the place where her rock sculptures hugged the shore. Where she might look out and frame anything she wanted through the crack between the smaller and bigger rock. He glanced at Allison again. Alas, she wasn't his type after all.

"Namaste," he said.

Love, Really

This is the part where he appears. It is simple. An *x*. He has "favorited" you. Then he "winks" at you, and finally he writes to you.

"You're so pretty," he types. You read that and look at his picture. There he is. It is like a small but tidy lightning bolt has hit you in the temple. Ka-zing. You have been struck. It was neatly done. You "wink" and "favorite" him back.

Imagine. That simple. Hit by lightning and yet left so whole and alive. And maybe, you are thinking, if it is possible, even improved upon. It is a healing lightning bolt. You go to sleep thinking that someone somewhere thinks you are pretty. And this someone, he is beautiful. You think that his face is like a country you visited long ago and were happy in. Maybe it was in another lifetime. You go to sleep smiling and in the middle of the night you have a dream that your body has developed the ability to hum.

This is the part where he comes to your door. You have avoided this for weeks. Partly because you are not sure you are as pretty in person as you are in your picture. But partly because you love that humming thing your body has learned how to do in your sleep; it is like you have developed your own personal motel magic fingers. You are afraid if you meet him that it will be lost.

"Hey," he says.

"Hey," you say back. His voice is like a beautiful, ragged engine. It has lived a long time in his throat—it turns out he is almost exactly your age—and it makes a sort of hoarse sound. It is a lived-in, been-there, done-that voice.

He has come to walk your dog with you. So you do. You get the leash and go outside to walk your dog. Your dog is very old and he notices this. The way he sort of stumbles on the curbs. The man notices that the dog's collar is very loose and that the dog could slip out of it any time, and almost does.

"Yeah," you say, "it is just an act we do, this *walking the dog* thing. We do it for the neighbors. They like us better this way."

The man laughs. It is a good and real laugh, a down-home meat-and-potatoes laugh, and you love it. The dog sniffs for a long time at a certain tree trunk. You stand there with this man, waiting, while the dog sniffs and pees and sniffs some more. You want to look at the man and see if he is the same him of the favoriting. The same him as the one who makes your body hum. You snatch a glance, small as a second. Small as a baby pea. And wonder of wonders: He is. The very same. Man.

This is the part where you make a plan. You will go out for a drink. You and the man. You are nervous. You are nervous because you like this man so much. He is a stranger but somehow not a stranger. He is, you think, the person you have been waiting to meet all your life. How could that be? That is ridiculous. You know that it is. But still. He is. He is waiting in the parking lot of the bar and you go in together. It is a slow night. You order beers and go to sit at a quiet corner table. Immediately you begin to talk and so does he. He tells you his life story, in an abbreviated fashion, of course. Wives, children, land, music. You tell him yours back. Job, dog, child, house. All the cards are laid out, face up, and you both look at them and somehow in the middle of this you have taken his hand and you are holding it. He is holding yours back and his is a hand you have been waiting to hold all your life. How could this be? It is ridiculous. But there it is. That same hand.

Revelation: Meeting the man does not stop your body from humming at night. In fact, your body is now a harmonica. You are trying out a few tunes with it. And you find it can improvise. It is a wise old magic-fingers harmonica, your body. What a thing. You would like to tell the man he has turned your body into a musical instrument but you are too shy, and besides, he might not entirely understand. But deep inside you suspect it; his body is humming too at night, when you are not there. The harmonica of him is playing the same songs, perhaps, and wouldn't that be crazy?

This is the part where you spend the night with the man. There is not a lot of discussion about this or planning. You just do and it is the most natural thing, so easy. All night long you kiss and touch and it is like you have been waiting for just this body to meet with yours, to consume and be consumed by you. It is just like that.

"Are you noticing it?" you finally ask. You do not say what it is, but it doesn't matter, because he nods and you think he might be crying a little. "I am noticing it," he says.

Some days you go to his house and you just sit there, side by side. If you touch it is like little lightning bolts all over now. And this is something, because you are over fifty years old and way beyond the lightning bolt stage of love, you think. When he kisses you and you kiss back it is like you are home. Home being the man himself. This is ridiculous, you think, as you hardly know this man. But there it is: home.

The man now knows a few real things about you. That not only do you have an old dog but you also have five cats. That you do not always clean your car. That you have a husband somewhere that you never see. That you have a child who does ballet. That you do not always wash your dishes immediately after you eat. The man says he must notice these things because he is trying to figure out if this thing of you, this reality of you, fits with the reality of him. He must look at you this way because he is practical, he says. "I am a logical guy," he chants. And while love is sweet, reality is very important. You take a look back at the reality of him. You notice he has the most beautiful hands. And at that exact moment he says: "You have the most beautiful hands."

When you try harder to see the reality of him you see that this man has no job. He has no health insurance and he lives in a faraway place. You notice that he has had many previous wives and that he, too, has a big dog. His dog is young, however, and he tells you that his dog can run up to thirty miles per hour. Your dog cannot do this. In fact, your dog probably can't run five miles per hour. There is a good chance your dog won't like the man's dog. And that must be what the man means by reality. Reality is when the man who makes little lightning bolts hit you all over and has turned your body into a harmonica at night has a dog that is smarter, younger, and faster than yours, and they might not get along.

This is the part where an old girlfriend shows up at the man's house. They must take a trip together to New York City, where she must do some work. This was planned, the man tells you, before you met. And you really don't have a commitment yet, anyway. Besides, he points out, you are married. The man and his old girlfriend go away for a weekend. While you understand that this was a planned thing, it feels bad, bad, bad. You think this has had an effect on the lightning bolts; they are changing now when they hit you all over. They are starting to get mean, they hurt in certain spots. One is right under your rib cage, a place you identify as where your heart must sit. But this is ridiculous, you think. Your actual heart, the organ of it, cannot possibly care about the man going to New York with this woman.

The man returns. He immediately calls you and tells you he is sad about this, what happened with the old girlfriend. She has left a lot of things at his house and some of them are dresses she will sell. She will come back for them soon. You tell a friend about this. The woman and her dresses. You tell her about the lightning bolts and how they have turned mean, and even painful.

"Hmmm," says your friend.

"Hmmm what?" you ask.

"Hmmm. Dresses," she replies. "Did you ask what sizes they are?"

Yes, your friend wants to know about the dresses, and how much they cost.

"They are butt ugly," you tell your friend, explaining you snuck in and opened one of the bags and looked at them one morning when the man was shaving.

"Ugly to you might be pretty to me," she says.

This is the part where the woman comes back for her dresses. She has to spend the night, apparently. But the man has told her the sleeping arrangements have changed. The woman says that is fine but you as a woman know this is bullshit. If you were this woman it would not be fine that the sleeping arrangements had changed. If you were her you would crawl right into bed with him after he was asleep. And, secretly, you imagine this is *just* what she did.

This is the part where you get upset. The woman with the dresses will come back again and again and again. The man says it is over between them, not to worry.

But you do. Your worry has become a drum that is much louder than the harmonica of you that plays when you are asleep. Sometimes it wakes you up and the humming— the beautiful humming—is completely drowned out by it. You have a fight with the man. You do not want the woman with the dresses to come back. "I will not be rude," he says. "I am not that kind of a person."

This is the part where the man tells you he loves you. It happens fast, a mumble really. Then louder. You want to savor it, because you think you also love this man, the whole gestalt of him, the familiar country that stretches from his face to his toes. But you realize it has flipped by before you can. It is a flip book of a sentence and before you can catch an image of this love, another image appears. The other image, interestingly, is of a dress. A butt-ugly dress.

This is the part where you make dinner with the man. You cook him enchiladas. You have sort of improvised the recipe based on one your mother used to use. Hers were good but yours are less good. You serve them and you can tell he doesn't really like them. You have already told him you cannot cook, but now you have dished him up the actual evidence. You are a woman with too many cats, a child, and an old dog. You are a woman who makes bad enchiladas. You can see it in his eyes. The bad enchilada maker of you. And you are beginning to suspect that the man is not feeling the humming at night anymore when he thinks of you. This makes you so sad.

This is the part where you write the man a letter. You write it by hand and it is very long. You drive to his house to read it to him. In it you talk about how much you hated it when he went away with the woman with the dresses. How much you like him and how confused you are by him. The man lies on his back with his eyes shut while you read him the letter. Afterward, he sighs. "What was the thesis sentence, and what was the conclusion?" he asks. "I am not sure I understand." Then he turns and takes hold of your foot. "I love you," he says. "I love your foot."

About all the rest, he just says something he often says: "It is what it is." And "I take one day at a time." You realize that you have heard those sentences before in an AA meeting you once went to with your sister. The beautiful man who loves you spouts many clichés like this. You wish he would be a bit more original.

This is the part where the lightning bolts turn into small dark hammers that pound on you. When you sleep, they come out of a red box and hammer away at you. They will not go back into their box, even though you have told them to. "Go away, you shitty little hammers," you say. One of the hammers turns to you and grows a mouth. "Make me," it says. You realize that you have no idea how to make the hammer go back into its red box. No idea at all. So you just sit there while they hammer at you, and you put your elbow up, over your face, to protect your eyes. It would be awful to lose an eye to a stupid little dream hammer.

This is the part where the man goes away for a long time and forgets to text. You are not even sure where he went. You text him: "I love you." Three days later you get a text back: "Luv u 2," he texts. All is well, you think, at least on paper. Or on screen.

This is the part where the woman comes back for the rest of her dresses. You are not happy about this, but what can you do? She will stay two days. Meanwhile, the lightning bolts and the humming have stopped. The hammers have gone away. Inside you now is a dead zone. A horse latitudes. You go to sleep and look at it, a big tepid lake that extends out from the side of your head, opens and opens. But it is not a friendly, swimming kind of lake. More of a large cesspool, actually. And nobody is taking any steps to clean it up.

You want to tell the man, *You are killing the humming. You are eradicating lightning, man! Be careful, you have created a lake of sorrow.* But this would sound odd, you realize, and might be one more thing that he could add to the long and ever-growing list of your flaws. Bad enchiladas, old dog, five cats, child. So you don't say a word. Whenever you see him he says, *I love you, I love you. You are so cute. I love your little toes. I love your face. I love your words. I love your brain.* And you want to drink in those words, you do, you want to pack up and move inside the house of them and live there, right there in their dictionary, to hell with your cats and dog and child; here is love, love! But the butt-ugly dresses are stopping you.

You want to believe in a future with the man. But the future is cloudy, like the lake that extends from your head now when you sleep is cloudy. You want to believe that love is strong. You want to believe. This is the part where you say you want to fix it, this thing of you. "Fix what?" he asks. "Nothing is broken." You realize that you and the man are having completely different experiences. You and he are not in the same love affair but in two separate ones. It is a mere coincidence that they happen to be with each other.

This is the part where you go back online to the romance website and see that the man has been very active there, in the time since you have met. This is the part where the place under your ribs sighs. This is the part where you cry. This is the part where you try to teach your mouth how to say it. How to say goodbye to a man who is a country where you wanted to emigrate. A man whose face was so familiar.

This is the part where you realize: It is what it is.

This is the part where you realize you will, in fact, take. One. Day. At. A. Time.

But then things change, yes! There is a sea change. The man says he has thought about it and he wants you no matter what. He is willing to take on the cats and dog and child. In fact, he wants to, he wants to be a family, by golly, and you are the one he wants to be a family with. You and yours. And you bring your dog over and, lo and behold, the dogs get along! And it doesn't matter that his dog is sleek and fast and yours is old and lumpy. There is a place on the rug where your dog settles right in and, with a little groan, falls asleep. He is happy at the man's house! He drinks from the man's dog's water dish. Slurp slurp slurp. And the man's dog doesn't even growl.

This is the part where he tells you he has made a commitment, sort of, he has gone off the website and told the woman with the dresses not to come back. She has had to come and get all the dresses. And then, it happens; he gives you a key to his house.

This is the part where you tell the man you are his. You will divorce that faraway husband. You will take a cooking class. Your old dog will settle in and live and die in the man's life and house. As for your child, she will be grown up soon. This is something that pinches your heart.

As for the five cats . . . well. What can you say? They will eventually die or run away or settle in somehow and sleep on pillows and in corner baskets and do cat things in his life, too. The cats are the price of being with you. The test.

He nods his head, the man. He sees it. The cat price tag. The old dog you love. Your child who is almost grown. And he will take it on, he thinks. He can do it. This, he sees, is the price tag, the actual price of love.

Your body has begun to hum again at night when you sleep, but it is a less pronounced humming, a muted harmonica, background for a film perhaps, or a faraway harmonica that seeps in on occasion. *It is what it is*, you think. Because you love this man, you love him really. And that sort of thing is rare rare rare, at this age. It is a dodo bird. A white Siberian tiger. You are lucky to have found it at all. It is ridiculous, really. You will take it.

The Hardness Test

"I am," Charlie said, "an ugly man. I hope that's not a problem for you."

It was not only a problem, but a conundrum. If Estelle answered the question honestly, she realized she might as well say: "I am, actually, a shallow woman. I do care that you are ugly. I hope that is not a problem for you."

Or, she could answer: "I hardly care at all about that."

But that would constitute a lie, no way to start a relationship. And starting a relationship was what Estelle was all about. She was thirty-eight years old, no spring chicken, as her mother liked to remind her. She had paid a forty-dollar fee to join an online community called Loveforreals.com, to find a mate, before "all her eggs went bad"—again, her mother's phrase. Her mother did not mince words.

In the universe of Loveforreals.com she had a new identity. She was not Estelle with dangerously old eggs, but Lovegrrl15. She liked the "grrr" in the middle, which bespoke both appetite and a certain feminist ethos she found very cleverly denoted.

She couldn't afford to be choosy at thirty-eight; she couldn't afford not to take every person quite seriously. Her mother was right. And ugly? What was ugly anyway? A word, it was just a word. It began at the back of your mouth and moved forward to your tongue. At the end of saying it you were practically smiling. (If you doubt this, try it.) She typed back: "Oh, don't be silly. You look fine in your profile picture. I am sure you are not ugly at all."

In fact, the man named Charlie had a very fuzzy, softly focused profile picture. He could look like anything at all. He could have a terribly misshapen head. He could be a hermaphrodite, a half-man, half-woman person. He could be one of those half-chicken people they have at the county fair. He could be a Mexican hairboy grown up. Estelle had read about the Mexican hairboy long ago in *Ripley's Believe It or Not*. This boy was covered—all over his body—with soft brown hair. It was as if he had been carpeted. But someone, somewhere, would love this carpeted man. They might be very happy.

Since this exchange, the word "ugly" had begun to grate on her. She had recently moved from a bucolic town in Connecticut to a very plain and sad little town in central New York named Horseheads. A place that certainly could be called "ugly," with its tired strip malls and neighborhoods that looked all worn out, like they wanted to just board up already and call it quits. Yet there was beauty there, too, as she constantly reminded herself. There was a lovely full-blown peony bush at the end of her street, Marcus Avenue, that looked like someone had detonated a purple tube of paint. And there was a marvelous weeping willow, right by the entrance to the park, a place where the local boys tore up the asphalt on their skateboards. Whizzing by, flipping in the air and looping on a concrete half-pipe that was the gift of some local good-deed doer, they reminded Estelle of electrons spinning around their atomic nuclei that she had seen in a textbook long ago, criss-crossing and loop-de-looping. They were fun to watch, skidding and clicking up and down, protected somehow by the shadows of those long wispy arms of willow. But she had a nervous feeling about them, too. Sooner or later something bad could happen there, willow or no.

Beauty is in the eye of the beholder, she repeated to herself, and asked Charlie, aka Mr. Ugly (she had begun to refer to him as such in her journal), to meet her for a drink. This was a very daring thing to do, but desperate times call for desperate acts, another quip she got from dear old Mom, who lived in Poughkeepsie, another not-so-beautiful place where there were little instances and inklings of beauty. There had been a beauty spotting just last Thursday, her mother said, when all the Red Hat ladies came out for a photo shoot in front of Mrs.

Goldenburg's rose garden. "Red hats, red roses, you should have been there," said her mother.

Yes, she should have, it must have been very cute, but then she lived far away and had a job as an office assistant at a meatpacking company, God Bless America Meats, that gave her great benefits and where her boss gave her Friday afternoons off all summer. How often do you get that at a job? It almost made living in Horseheads, New York, worthwhile, although a Friday afternoon off there was hard to enjoy. She could drive one town over to Elmira and go to the movies, or drive over to Corning and visit the glass museum. But how many times could a person go to a glass museum, even if it is very, very good? It was a finite number. She was sure.

It had recently occurred to her that a woman who is an office assistant at a meatpacking plant in a town named Horseheads at age thirty-eight really can't be picky at all. She was lucky Charlie even wrote her back. So the date was set; it would be cocktails and conversation. And that would be that. If they "clicked," it could become more. If not, then nothing much would be lost but another evening of her life.

As the date grew nearer for Estelle and Charlie, the self-described Ugly Man, to meet, Estelle became more nervous. What would she do if he had been in one of those car accidents that rearrange your face so you look like a Picasso painting? What if he had a hunchback? What if he was covered in boils, or had acne pits so deep that you could fit a fingertip inside them? She pondered how she would politely extricate herself from such a person, and what sort of person it would make her if she did—just fled like that.

"I am so excited to meet you," wrote Charlie, two days before the evening of their date. Estelle felt a chill run down her spine. It wasn't the good kind of chill, the excited and slightly nervous romantic sort, but the other sort, the kind you get when you know you are soon to have oral surgery and it could necessitate some sort of large metal instruments sawing away inside your mouth. "I am excited, too," she wrote back.

She was becoming a liar. The Ugly Man was making her one.

One evening before the date, which was set for seven o'clock at the Black Bay Tavern in a neighboring town, Estelle saw she had a message on Loveforreals .com. It was from someone with the screen name "Handsomeguy345."

What are the chances, she thought, *that someone screen-named "Handsomeguy345" would e-mail you just as you are about to meet an ugly man?* It was a million to one, perhaps. It was like winning a lottery. That rare. But without the money, of course.

"Like your profile," wrote the handsome man. "Wanna chat?"

"Hi there," Estelle wrote back.

And the conversation proceeded from there:

Handsomeguy345: I like your smile.

Lovegrrl15: Thanks!

Handsomeguy345: So whereabouts do you live?

Lovegrrl15: Horseheads. Where do you live?

Handsomeguy345: Corning.

Lovegrrl15: Oh, I like that glass museum there.

Handsomeguy345: Yeah, it's real good. So what do you do in Horseheads?

Lovegrrl15: I work at God Bless America Meats.

Handsomeguy345: Oh wow, I like their meat. It's real good.

Lovegrrl15: I know, I get free steaks once a month. And I get Friday afternoons off in the summer.

Handsomeguy345: How lucky.

Lovegrrl15: I know.

Handsomeguy345: We should get together one of those Fridays. Maybe go to the glass museum? They have a nice café.

Lovegrrl15: I love that café!

Handsomeguy345: Then it's a date.

With that, Estelle found herself in the most awkward and peculiar position she imagined could possibly exist. A date with both an ugly and a handsome man, one day apart. Drinks with Ugly Man followed by lunch with Handsome Man at a glass museum, no less. "What are the chances?" she asked Margaret, her coworker, the bookkeeper at God Bless America Meats. Margaret had recommended she go on Loveforreals.com. She had met Jake there and now they were engaged. She called him Jakey-poo and talked to him on the phone in baby talk. "Awww," Estelle could hear her coo, "is Jakey-poo upset? Does Jakey-poo need a huggy wuggy?"

Estelle had heard people talk to their children like this and found it very annoying, but with a boyfriend it was even worse. She wondered if all the couples who met on Loveforreals.com developed annoying methods of address. You meet someone in print, how can you know what they sound like in audio?

"You can't know," her mother said. "Deal with it. You are pushing forty."

"Technically," Estelle said, "I am one year away from pushing forty."

"What-ev-er!" her mother replied. It was something you would expect to hear from a teenager, not a sixty-something woman living in Poughkeepsie who belongs to the Red Hat Society. Estelle suspected she got the phrase from her niece, LaDonna, who was living with her mother while her sister, Sonia, was in rehab. Sonia had been a crackhead and now everyone was very happy she was just a pillhead, addicted to Darvon and Valium and such. "It is so much easier to get off of those," her mother said.

But Estelle knew the truth, that Sonia was taking their mother's Oxycontins, prescribed for severe osteoporosis that had caused her back to curve up like a question mark. She would crush them up in the bathroom and snort the resulting powder. She was also taking their mother's fentanyl patches and sucking on them, under her tongue like a lozenge. These were not good things, not at all, but she hid her sister's secret practices the way you might hide a vibrator in a drawer, even liking that her sister had found a source of relief, and meanwhile let their mother pick on her, the good daughter. The one who held down a job, had recently acquired a mortgage, and had never given birth to a child because she felt it was unethical without the means to create a college fund immediately for said child. You couldn't go reproducing in the world just because you had a job that provided the occasional free steak. She let her mother rip her to shreds, whenever possible. It was like a favor to Sonia. And she owed her one.

It had to do with something that had happened long, long ago, to her sister, and the role Estelle had played in it. The event was so distant and truly dark it almost seemed like a movie she had once seen, or a dream. But it was real and she knew it and it was like a stone in her heart, a hard cold spot there that never let her feel completely happy.

She recalled the geology classes she had taken in high school and how they had a hardness scratch test you could perform on rocks, to find out what sort of minerals the different rocks held inside them. The MOH Hardness Scale would tell you if rocks were made of more than one mineral. She recalled they had tested for

(1) fluorite, (2) gypsum, (3) calcite, (4) quartz. You could find out things about rocks by determining what other material could scratch them and what they could scratch. She thought if you scratched that rocky place in her heart with a penny, a paper clip, or even a diamond chip, you would never see a scratch. It was that hard. It probably contained molybdinum or uranium or something. Or maybe even an element that had never been discovered. Her heart contained a glob of Kryptonite, the stuff that made Superman vulnerable, that had been imported by a meteor from a faraway world where things were harder than any substance known to man. Her sister's heart, on the other hand, was more like a fossil. Something that had once been an organic thing, but had died out. A species gone extinct. Her heart was a dodo bird, or a small dinosaur, that had once run very fast. Estelle had played a part in it, the killing of that fast, special heart.

When she was nine and Sonia was seven, they had gone to a camp where each girl had to care for and tend her own horse. Estelle's was Frost, a tall white gelding. But Sonia had gotten Kit, and Kit was pregnant. Halfway through camp Kit foaled and was out of commission, so when the camp girls went on their daily trail ride, up over the rise and into the hills for the entire morning, Sonia had to stay behind with Gramps, the father of one of the counselors. One afternoon Sonia had told Estelle that the old man would touch her in her underpants and smelled bad, "like sour cheese."

"I wanna go home," she told her sister, a tear dripping off the end of her nose onto her lip, where it quivered for a moment, before it fell.

Estelle, painfully aware of the position both girls already had in the complicated popularity echelon of the camp, had seen this as a further risk to their reputation, her sister drawing additional negative attention to them. Making some sort of stink about wanting to go home would be bad for their positioning; it could even rub off on her, and she was just getting in with the cool crowd.

"We can't go home, Mom will get mad at us," she had told Sonia, ignoring her little sister's tears. "And whatever you do, don't tell anyone about this but me."

The following day, as the long column of girls rode away upon their horses, Estelle looked back. It was just a glance, but long enough to see Sonia's face, wild with fear, as the old man placed his hand on her shoulder and guided her away.

Since that day, it seemed to Estelle, Sonia had shifted inside, her rare heart had fossilized and she had departed from life. And her own heart had gotten that stone inside it. That chip of Kryptonite that hardened her, and made it possible for her to take any sort of critique their mother could dole out. She deserved it, after all.

The day of her first date, the one with Ugly Man Charlie, soon arrived. Estelle found herself going repeatedly into the bathroom at God Bless America Meats, not to actually use the bathroom but to look at herself in the mirror. It was, in fact, a kind mirror; she rather liked the way she looked in it. There were mean and there were kind mirrors in the world, Estelle had discovered. The mirrors at the mall in Binghamton were quite cruel and made her look obese and hideous. The mirrors at the airport there, on the other hand, were quite sweet to her, much better than she deserved; whenever she was going on a trip she looked forward to the way she looked in them, kind of cute and youthful and travelly. But the waist-up mirror in God Bless America Meats was the kindest of all. She always looked stunning in it, like a real beauty. It made her days working there so much more pleasant knowing, at any moment, she could go into the bathroom and look that way. It would make it hard to ever leave the job, in fact, because leaving would mean leaving that image of herself, the really pretty girl one, a girl who seemed like a fine-looking and even good person in the world, behind.

She let the door slam behind her and stood there a moment, in the soft white light of an overhead bulb (overhead bulbs are much better than fluorescent ones!), looking at the girl in the mirror who was going to have a drink in three hours with the Ugly Man, Charlie. She was *such* a pretty girl there. But she knew, deep inside her heart, somewhere next to that hard cold spot, that she could also be an ugly girl herself, a girl who had left her own sister behind. She would be ugly if she were just looking at herself at the Oakdale Mall rather than the bathroom mirror at the meat company. She could not afford to be choosy. She was lucky to have a date at all.

"So what are you wearing?" asked her mother, in a cell phone text.

"MOM! Stop!" she texted back.

"Okay, don't tell me, but it better not be anything green or yellow, those are NOT your colors."

Her mother had begun texting recently, something her niece, LaDonna, had introduced to her. And like a teenage girl, it seemed dear Mom could not get enough of it. She texted several times a day: Did you check oil? Did you find a good dentist yet in town? Would you like my dentist to give a reference?

"I am fine, Mom. I have a dentist. I do not need a reference. I had the oil changed."

"Well don't change the oil too often, it is a waste of money, they say you only need to every twenty-five thousand miles."

"Okay, Mom, I may have had it changed a bit too soon."

She would cop to mistakes often like that; it was something she did for her sister. A sort of recompense for that thing that had happened, long ago. She would let her mother go off on her for this or that small thing to save her sister the scrutiny that might reveal her

Oxycontin addiction and the thing about the patches, the way she sucked on them until she was fairly loopy with narcotic.

At 4:30, Estelle went into the bathroom one last time and looked at her reflection. There she was again, a pretty woman. She applied a little spray mist cologne. Something called Butterfly Mist she had picked up at Walmart. It reminded her of Coco by Chanel, which was far too expensive. She coiffed her hair a bit with a finger. Pulling a ringlet out into several. *I am pretty. I may even be too pretty to date this ugly man, but there are reasons why I should be with an ugly man, too*, she thought, just as the little ding went off on her phone. "I hope you aren't considering canceling your date," her mother texted. "You are running out of time, sweetie."

She turned off her phone and walked out to her desk. There stood Margaret. "You sure are using the bathroom a lot today," she said. "Everything okay?"

"Oh, yes," Estelle said. "I'm just nervous about a date I have tonight."

"Really? A date? With who?"

"Oh, I don't really know," she said. "I met him online."

"Well, as you know, that is where I met Jake . . . and look at us now . . . We are practically married!"

"Yes," Estelle said. "I know."

The hour of the drink date arrived and Estelle settled into her car to drive to the meeting place, feeling a bit like a princess about to head to the ball. But it was sort of an anti-ball, she thought, knowing that the prince was an ugly man. Oh well, she thought, her car was nice. She had recently washed it and hung up a pine-tree-shaped car deodorizer that smelled, enigmatically, like butterscotch. She popped in her favorite CD. It was the Clash, *London Calling*, and with its familiar lyrics singing to her, she drove at medium speed to the bar where they were set to meet.

There, parked in front, was a tired old Saab with a dog in the back. Standing beside it was a disheveled man in sweatpants, with one leg rolled to the knee and the other rolled down. *It couldn't be? Could it?* she thought. It was. Her date, the Ugly Man. "You're late," he said as she stepped out of her car, "but I will let it go this time." He cracked a smile and Estelle could see he meant this as a sort of humor. She smiled weakly back. He introduced her to his dog, Belinda, who was a very old-looking dog, with a wounded-looking left leg. Together they walked into the bar. He ordered them each a beer. "You must try the stout," he said. "It is very good."

"I don't like stout," she said.

"You will like this one," said Charlie.

It annoyed her, the idea that someone might think they knew her tastes better than she did. But when Estelle tasted the beer she had to admit she did like it. Surprisingly. She never liked such beers, but this one had a deeply nutty taste. It was like drinking liquid macadamia nuts with a hint of oak.

"Yummy," she said, despite herself.

"Told ya," said Charlie.

They sat and chatted for a while and decided to go for a drive to see the moon rise over a particular spot that he knew of, where a "lovely vista" could be seen. *He will probably try to kiss me there,* Estelle thought, annoyed by the cliché of it all.

While he drove, she found herself searching the man's face to pinpoint exactly where his ugliness lay. She wanted to zero in on it, hone in like radar. If his ugliness was a code, she thought she should try to crack it, get to the bottom of it. It would be nice to define it more closely. But when she did look closer at him, she found she could not. He actually had a nice nose, rather pretty green eyes, a strong jaw, lovely skin, Charlie. It was the way it all fit together that was wrong. It just didn't. He was sort of asymmetrical. She recalled once reading about a study of infants that demonstrated that they would go more readily to a stranger who had symmetrical features. Charlie was off-kilter. That was his ugliness, she decided. If she focused on one element at a time in his face, she found him quite tolerable, attractive even.

They drove toward the beautiful vista place slowly, and he pointed out places he knew in the town. "I used to work at that bank," he said. "One summer I made ice cream cones at that stand." He had grown up there and the whole world seemed a map of his life.

They heard a siren. Charlie pulled over to the side of the road and let an ambulance pass by. "Wonder where it's going," he muttered, and she realized that wherever it was he had probably had some important experience right there, as a child. It was a very smallish town. They didn't have to wonder long. The ambulance pulled into the parking lot near the skate park; nearby a skateboarder lay in the middle of a ring of people looking on, as if his apparent injury were an exotic animal they might never get an opportunity to see again. A wildebeest, perhaps, or one of those all-white tigers. The EMTs popped out of the ambulance and pushed their way through the crowd. Estelle and Charlie, at an adjacent stop light, looked on at the spectacle as well. Just before the light changed, another boy on a skateboard stepped over to the cars in line at the light and announced, like it was his duty: "He was trying to flip over on the half-pipe," he said, "do a one-sixty: I told him not to, but he wouldn't listen."

"A lot of people were opposed to that skate park," the Ugly Man told her, after the light changed and they had driven away.

"Were you?" she asked, feeling shaken and horrified by the scene.

"Was I what?"

"Opposed to the skate park?"

"Oh, I don't know," he said.

Soon they were at the bluff where Charlie said the beautiful vista was to be seen. They pulled up to a spot and parked, but it was cloudy, you couldn't see much at all. Somewhere, behind the fogginess, Charlie promised, a lovely view was lurking. Estelle found it annoying, to drive a distance to see something obscured, even if it was beyond his control.

In addition, she had just discovered that she herself looked very plain in Charlie's rearview mirror, which she had used to check her lipstick. She thought she could see crow's-feet fanning out from her eyes, something she had never really noticed before as so unsightly. In the distance she could hear the ambulance siren singing mournfully as it ferried the skateboarder to medical treatment, probably in Elmira.

Charlie, the Ugly Man, did not try to kiss her. This was both a relief and annoying, which, Estelle realized, was the sort of reaction only a person with a Kryptonite heart could have.

The next day Estelle woke up with a dream still freshly planted in her mind. It was about her sister, Sonia. They were girls again, and her sister was angry at her. "Estelle did it, Momma," she sobbed, pointing at a broken doll. "She killed Lillith."

Her dream mother glared at her, angrily. "You will have to give her one of your dolls, now, Estelle."

She had woken up feeling queasy from this dream. But then she remembered. It was the day of her lunch date with the beautiful man. She was going to Corning, to the glass museum café. And she was running late. She had overslept.

"Are you up?" texted her mother, whom she had told about the drink date but not the lunch date. "How was it?"

She was so groggy from sleep that at first she wasn't sure exactly what her mother was talking about. She thought for a second that her mother might have found some way to get into her dreams and was asking about the dream about the doll. *How was the dream? How was the doll?* Then it hit her: Her mother was asking about Charlie. About the drink date the evening before.

"Fine," she texted back. "I tried stout beer and liked it, but then we saw a kid get hurt bad at a skate park."

"Well did he ask you out again? Did he seem to like you?"

"Mom," she texted, "it is Saturday morning. I haven't even had coffee yet."

"That is immaterial," her mother texted. "A complete non sequitur."

She put down the phone and went into the bathroom. There stood a perfectly okay-looking version of herself; that woman in Charlie's rearview mirror—the unkissed woman—was just some sort of strange anomaly. After all, those mirrors were so bad they came with those odd disclaimers about "objects in mirrors," and all that. They were known to be flawed, it was official.

She put on a pretty, flowered pink-and-yellow top and drove to Corning. It was a beautiful morning, and feathery clouds seemed flung up in the sky gaily. She stopped for a coffee at the gas station convenience store. She liked hers with Irish cream "whitener" in it, which came from little flavored creamers in a bin next to the coffee pot. As she pulled off the top, her eyes grazed the adjacent newspaper stand. A headline pounced off the front page: "Skateboarder killed in freak accident at Horseheads Park."

"He died? The kid last night? Actually died?"

"Yep," said the convenience store manager, a guy with a nametag that said "Hi, I'm Alan."

"He is dead all right."

Her stomach caved. She bit her lip. It seemed so extreme just then—death by skateboard, almost impossible really, and to think she had been right there, probably right after it happened.

She felt a bit guilty. Should a person really go to have lunch with a handsome man right after seeing someone killed? Was this part of a pattern in her life of looking the other way rather than acknowledging terrible things? The Kryptonite-hearted girl thing? She paid at the register, took her coffee, got in her car and drove fast, leaving the headline behind her as quickly as possible. She left off the radio and CD player. She just wanted to get there.

When she pulled into the vast parking lot at Corning, at the glass museum, she saw a man standing next to a BMW convertible, just standing there, completely still. He waved her over.

"Estelle!" he said. "Right here."

He was saving her a parking spot right next to him by literally standing in it. She pulled in and he stepped over and opened her car door. "Hello there!" he said.

Side by side they walked into the Corning Museum of Glass (he was a member, they didn't even have to pay) and into the little café. "You should see the new exhibit. Depression glass, it's beautiful," he said.

"Oh, I love that, red and pink, right?"

"And blue, they made dark blue."

She searched the handsome man's face. She was trying hard to locate his beauty, to zero in on it the way she had the ugly man's ugliness. She tried to look at each feature of him, one by one, without being too obvious. His eyes were ordinary brown eyes, nothing special about them. His nose was actually a little large. And he was balding. He was definitely balding. Once he took off his baseball cap (Red Sox—he was one of *those*, she thought, realizing she had detected that slight Bostonly accent on the phone the one time they spoke), she saw the absence of hair. Why did balding men always wear baseball caps? It merely drew attention to their baldness. Funny, she thought, the Ugly

Man had a full head of thick blond hair. This thing, beauty, it wasn't about features. It was the way they were assembled! The Handsome Man was like a puzzle that had been put together right. Each plain feature complemented the rest. What a revelation it was, to finally actually comprehend beauty.

Just then Isaac, the Handsome Man, reached across the table confidently and took Estelle's hand, which was holding a steaming cup of tea. "I have been waiting so anxiously to meet you. All week," he said, "I waited. And you are just as beautiful as I imagined."

"Wow," she said, feeling at that moment like the version of herself in the mirror at God Bless America Meats, not the airport mirror version and certainly not the Oakdale Mall version, not the car rearview mirror and not the girl she had once been. A woman who could be a new person, not the one who had left behind a sister to a terrible fate. "So sweet. Thank you."

Somewhere, right at that moment, while Estelle parsed the beauty in the handsome man and the handsome man parsed the beauty in Estelle, she thought the Ugly Man, Charlie, might be walking his dog, Belinda. Somewhere else, the family of the skateboarder was beginning the arduous process of planning their boy's funeral. Open or closed casket? White roses? Nosegay or small spray inside the casket? And her sister, Sonia, was reaching a trembling hand into her mother's medicine cabinet toward the package of fentanyl patches.

She would extract one and place it under her tongue, a temporary answer to her thirty-year-old pain. And somewhere far, far away, a meteor made of the hardest material in the universe was wending its way through space, plummeting through the cold dark of nothingness, toward Earth. A hardness that would even make the hard and lonely place inside Estelle seem soft, light, and malleable.

Limerence

T here was an everything and then there was a something.

This something that had invaded Larry's heart appeared to have brought a suitcase. It had unpacked and left its socks and underwear and hairbrush out. It clearly intended to stay. It didn't care about all the things that he had previously done or cared about. It was a selfish something and wanted every acre, hectare, and mile of him.

The something chased the everything away.

Some days, Larry liked the something, let it tell him stories and play out elaborate filmstrips in his mind of lovely situations. Other days it was mean to him and taunted him with feelings of rejection and loss. He was completely owned by it; it had him.

And that was a feeling he did not like. No, not at all.

"Blame it on the Internet," said his therapist, Jonathan. "You should avoid going on at all costs." Larry had admitted to himself that he was addicted to the Internet and meeting people on it, which was why he had sought psychological counseling. In addition, once a week he went to a support group Jonathan had told him of. The support group met in a rather dingy room in a Methodist church. People sat in uncomfortable chairs around two long tables that had been pushed together to make a larger table, and they went around the room saying the first half of the Serenity Prayer, and then each one responded with a brief anecdote about how something in their lives felt out of control and how they were working on it. All the people in the support group were owned by the something. They felt helpless and wanted someone there or everyone there to jump right in and tell them what to do or just say "I get that," or "You are not alone." He liked the support group because everyone in it had met the something and seen how it could be so disrespectful of them. They would sit in a circle and talk, talk, talk, talk, talk about the something, with brief breaks for coffee and cigarettes. You would have thought these people were strung out on heroin. But they were not. It was the something. It was like a drug but it was not a drug.

In Larry's case the something had a specific name: Louise. She had found him there in the ether of the magical darkness of online love, and the beginning was so innocent. "Like your smile," Louise wrote.

Such an innocuous little compliment. Such a tiny sentence even. Three words long. It was barely a sentence. It had a verb, "like," and a noun, "smile," and then there was that complicated and oh-so-very-stabbingly personal pronoun, "your." How many times had that sentence been reviewed? It was uncountable. The sentence was turned inside out and then back outside in, and flipped over to see if there was any mud on its feet. It had had its hair combed and its pockets searched for loose change. It had had its passport stamped for future travel purposes and it had even possibly been proposed to, that little sentence. It was more than any sentence could bear, and finally it had broken into pieces, under all that pressure.

"Leave me alone," the sentence finally said to Larry. And he had tried. He really had. He even threw it into his computer trash with the spam. But then he got it out again and kept it in a special folder, labeled "Louise"— which was a very dangerous and haunting place indeed.

Who would have guessed that such a small, small sentence would grow into this something? It was like the seed Jack planted that turned into the beanstalk. Jack had to climb up it, remember? There was no backing down once that thing sprouted.

Larry was a man who spent much of his days in an office, busy with papers and files and folders, and while he had always felt quite busy before, he found that there was a lot of time in between various tasks to give pause to the sentence. Somehow that sentence was able to grow and morph, a living thing, with bones and a rib cage and ideas about life.

He actually met this Louise (bar, two martinis, moonlit walk, she gave him a stick of gum, spearmint) and he found her to be pretty, smart, funny as all get out, and very romantic. She took his hand in hers without hesitation and it felt warm and full of heart there, like a small ticking bird. "Now that was a great kiss," she said, when their lips met briefly after this date. Then, when they kissed again, in a deeper way that involved a pressureful hug and something small that happened with their tongues, his heart did a little back flip like the kind kids did off the diving board at the public pool when he was a teenager. He himself had not been a back flip–doing boy, so he was quite astounded that his emotions could so boldly leap off the board of a moment like that.

That was the beginning. Louise and Larry hung out a number of times after that. Here is a list of what they actually did, for the purpose of accuracy:

1. They went out to eat.

    Larry: sausage stromboli, approximately six bites. He found his appetite had slunk away somewhere during the third one. Three beers.

Louise: broccoli cheddar soup; she ate it all and ordered dessert. Chocolate mousse cake. Ate it all and ordered coffee. Three beers and a shot.

2. They went to a movie at an art-house theater. *Casablanca*, a movie that, in time, Larry came to believe was not actually about a bar in Morrocco in World War II, but about the way the something could abduct people wholly from reality, pretty much eclipsing all else, even wartime circumstances. (Think about it: There is a very horrific thing going on with Nazis and a sad and crazy thing about letters of transport being sold on the black market that pretty much meant life or death to the holders. But all you, the viewer, care about is whether Rick and Ilsa will get it on.) Larry held Louise's hand but it got a bit sweaty there and she removed it and rather conspicuously wiped her hand off on her pant leg, which was a somewhat embarrassing moment.

3. Made spaghetti at Louise's house and ate it on her porch.

    (Larry, approximately four bites; Louise, two bowls and then a dish of coconut almond ice cream—she was not fat, by the way, just very hungry.) This meal was followed by a wild sexual interlude in Louise's bedroom that involved kisses all over Larry's body and a one-and-a-rather-breathless-half-hour lovemaking session.

4. One more wildly vigorous sexual encounter, two weeks later, again at Louise's house.

Three beers each. A bit of weed. A little talking, sweetly, then straight to the sex. Less passionate and a little quicker with abrupt motions and even a kind of cruelty and quasi-violence in the middle, followed by very warm hugs and kisses after. Larry actually spent the night. When he woke up he saw Louise sitting next to him, looking at him.

"Hi," he said.

She looked at him and he thought she might be looking right through him, using X-ray vision, like Superman had, to see what was behind and beyond him.

"Hi," she said.

He wondered how long she had been doing that, watching him. Her long red hair was loose and hung in ringlets around her face and she was naked. All around her was a bright glow from the sun, rising outside, filtered with many minute particles of dust, and he had a thought that she looked like an angel, ringed in a halo, and the dust motes looked at that moment quite shiny and un-dustlike. They looked like stars. That was it: She was encrusted in stars.

"Want breakfast?" he asked.

"Gotta go to work," she said, "sorry."

That is what happened. These are the actual facts. Now, on to the fuzzy part, where the something got out of control and became quite large and then grew teeth.

Minutes became hours became miles became rivers became oceans. Contact with Louise, she of the red-gold, star-encrusted hair, was sporadic at best and Larry found himself tabulating and analyzing them, the way you might analyze the gross national product of a country, say Peru. The Peru of Louise was complicated and demanded constant attention. Larry, who liked to work out at a local gym, found himself too tired to go for his ritual morning stint there. He was busy thinking about Louise.

Larry also had a dog, Homer. He had previously spent a lot of time with Homer, walking him, playing with him—he had coached him into a range of impressive Frisbee retrieval stunts. After meeting Louise, this time was cut short and finally abandoned altogether. The Frisbee fetching that had brought both he and the dog, a black Lab stray he adopted from a local shelter, such delight, seemed less delightful to him somehow. And why walk a dog when one has a rather large backyard the dog can wander around in on his own? It seemed less invigo-rating to walk and play with him, and he was busy now, thinking about when Louise might text or call him.

Homer, for his part, had become a different kind of dog. A barking and whining sort of dog who was most unpleasant to be around. "Sit, Homer, quiet!" he barked at his dog.

By spring, when he had not heard from Louise in over two weeks, he became quite despondent. He would flip through the Louise file on his computer, over and over. In it were all their texts, including the original sentence about the smile, which he had fished out of the trash and placed in there. Most of the texts were quite bland.

Then came a time when he would text her daily. "Just saying hi." "Howdy there." "Whussup stranger?" To these he received no reply at all. That was even more unsettling.

The sun was out more during this time and the days were longer and filled with more Louise-like silence and the annoying chatter of birds. Homer was more rest-less than ever. This was the time of year when he most enjoyed chasing squirrels and sniffing intensely at the bottoms of trees and certain clumps of grass. He would bark ceaselessly. He would run around the house from window to window, watching the squirrels leap from branch to branch. Larry was becoming terribly annoyed by these antics, and more than ever he felt as if he was walking in a stew of molasses.

What was Louise doing? Why didn't she write him back? Most important: What had he done wrong?

The something was fully grown now, and had sprouted hairs. On some mornings it had horns and yellow eyes. It lived in every room of his house now. It got in the car with him in the morning and went to his office and left with him.

Sometimes he would read it, that first sentence, and then go into his bathroom and look at his smile. It was a nice smile, he thought. But what had gone wrong from there? Had he not smiled that smile Louise liked enough? Had he been too serious? Too shy? Too forward? Not used enough deodorant?

He was attending the support group religiously at this point because he felt the people in the room in the Methodist Church understood him, understood his *predicament*. They nodded when he spoke; one older woman made a clucking noise with her tongue. Another time, a young girl came over to him after the meeting and asked him, point blank, "Are you all right?"

What did she mean by that, this girl? She couldn't have been more than eighteen. She herself had confided that she was addicted to Facebook. She went on it all times of the day and night and was very upset and a little bit sick when her mother hid her cell phone for a day. During the meetings he often saw her reach into her bag and take out her cell phone to quickly check it. Her thumbs, busying away at the keyboard, moved so fast they actually blurred. He often saw younger people doing this. Texting while walking down the street, while sitting at a red light in traffic. At restaurants.

This girl had a problem! Yet she seemed to think he had an even greater problem. One that necessitated a special and private conversation. Did he have such a problem?

Well, yes, he did. It was summer and the something that had abducted his old everything had become a new everything. There was no minute that went by when he did not want to check his cell phone or his e-mail inbox, or rake over the text messages in the Louise file.

Jonathan, the therapist, was quite concerned that these feelings had not subsided, and he was particularly disturbed to hear that Larry had begun driving by Louise's house, sometimes several times a day. "Some people might call this stalking, Larry," he said.

"But I don't knock on her door," Larry protested.

"Doesn't matter," said Jonathan. "The definition of stalking is quite broad. This behavior fits into it, I think."

Two people were concerned. Jonathan and the eighteen-year-old girl in the support group. Add to this

Larry's mother. "I never hear from you," she said, on the phone. "This isn't like you. Are you okay?"

Add to these his next-door neighbor, Barry. That made four people who were concerned. But Barry's concern was a bit more like anger. Barry thought Larry might be abusing Homer. He had seen him strike Homer on several occasions in a violent way. And Larry left Homer outside on a very short tether for entire days, without enough water. "Homer is fine," Larry insisted. "He has water!"

"Larry, honestly, this barking is driving us nuts."

Barry was an "us" with a woman named June. June seemed nice enough. She was pretty and smiled a lot and reminded him of Louise a bit. The way she held Barry's hand sometimes when they went out for a walk was like the time he and Louise had held hands. Come to think of it, most women reminded him of Louise. They weren't as awesome, of course.

Now that the something had become an everything, Larry was quite unable to do much else. He skipped breakfast, noshed on dried peanuts for lunch, and made himself a bowl of cereal for dinner. The dirty bowls were stacked in his sink. He didn't tidy up the way he used to, and, embarrassingly, there were some messes Homer had made that were still sitting there around the house. One day he noticed one was covered in flies.

It was midsummer and quite hot, so the messes had begun to smell and Larry himself had begun to smell, too. Jonathan mentioned this at a session. "When was the last time you showered, Larry?" he asked.

Larry considered the question. He was sure he had showered sometime but the days and times and activities blurred. He looked at his personal planner, a book that up until March was crammed with notes and scratched-out appointments, which was now oddly empty. He could not pinpoint a date for this showering question.

"Larry," said Jonathan. "I believe you are suffering from limerence."

"Limerence?"

"Yes. I think you have a pretty obvious case of it. Read this."

He handed Larry a paper on the topic. It was a long and turgid thing, filled with words he didn't know. "Can't you just sum this up for me, doc?"

"I have been thinking hard about this thing you are going through and I am pretty sure this is it. Limerence is an obsessive, unrequited love. It is actually a disorder. A disease, if you will. I will write you a scrip for a new antidepressant. The last one wasn't helping enough; this one should."

The something that had become an everything had a name!

"But how long does it take to get rid of this disease?"

"Well, the good news is, it does go away, most of the time. The bad news is, it can take up to two years."

Larry liked the idea that he had contracted a disease. It was not a disease called Louise. it was a disease called limerence. All day long he repeated it: Limerencelimerencelimerencelimerencelimerencelimerencelimerencelimerencelimerence.

It was August and quite hot out when Larry woke one morning, covered in sweat, to find Homer chewing on a shoe. He wasn't just chewing, however. Larry realized that Homer was actually eating the shoe. At that moment the thought of Louise, encrusted in stars, was trying to force its way into his thoughts, pushing out the sight of Homer eating a shoe. But then the word, the newfound name of the everything, popped into his mind and pushed Louise away. "Limerence," he said.

Homer stopped chewing the shoe and looked up at him, as if to say *Yes, dude, run with that thought.*

Larry got up and made his bed and got in the shower. He got out and got dressed and made himself breakfast. He was in the mood for eggs. When he got to his kitchen he was sort of surprised to find clutter everywhere. He hadn't seen that the night before. He opened his dishwasher and started loading it up. Then he added soap and realized he was actually enjoying the chugging sound the machine made as it churned the soap and hot water onto his dirty cereal bowls. He threw in a load of laundry and, again, enjoyed the sound the machine made, spinning and whirring away at the dirty clothes that lay in mounds around his house. He got a roll of paper towels and some spray cleaner and picked up several unpleasant mounds of dog doo. "Homer, you bad bad boy," he said. Homer barked and looked a bit sorry for it, he thought.

After eating his eggs and rinsing his dishes he got the leash and took Homer for a walk. By this time the wet clothes were in the dryer, and he enjoyed the hot dryer air exhaled from the side of the house into the morning. "Limerence," he said.

The morning seemed to like the word. It rewarded him with the sight of blooming rose bushes. "Limerence," he said to the roses. He greeted the neighbor with a nod and a smile. "Hi, Barry," he said. Barry grunted.

Homer strained against his leash, delighted to smell all the smells of the world. Dog pee, cat spray, squirrel essence, garbage, grass, small bugs inhabiting the grass. He felt infected by Homer's enthusiasm, and the walk they took was farther afield than any walk before.

A woman he once worked with drove by and waved at him. "Limerence," he mouthed.

When he got home he took his new antidepressant medication and scrubbed for a good long time at the bathtub, which had become gray with soot and stains.

He realized around noon that he had not looked at the Louise file one time, and the very thought of doing so turned his stomach a bit. "Limerence," he said. He drove to work by a new route and specifically did not drive by Louise's house. He got to work and had an unusually productive day, which was a good thing, since there were unattended files and papers all over his desk. He spoke to his computer, which he did not use to go online and check his personal e-mail. "Limerence," he said.

That week at the support group meeting, he hardly felt like sharing, but the leader called him out. "So how is it going with you, Larry?" he asked.

All eyes in the room turned to him. The old woman who clucked, the eighteen-year-old girl who was concerned, the guy with a tattoo of Jesus on his neck, and someone he had never noticed before, a very pretty lady in a dark-blue dress. "There is a name for the thing," he said. "I found out it is like a disease. It is called limerence."

"What is that?" the leader asked.

"It's complicated. Look it up."

The room went silent and everyone made a mental note. *Look up "limerence."*

Larry had looked it up and read about it for hours. Limerence was apparently a biological thing that can happen to people on occasion. There were statistics about it. Twenty percent of all people would go through it at some time in their lives. He just loved that there was math involved. Things with math had substance. They were actual.

Limerence erased the very small sentence that had grown so large. It had pushed the four dates into a corner and swept them into a dustbin. It had taken all the uncomfortable and troubling silences and spun them in the air into a small and quite pretty rainbow. And then the rainbow flew out the window. Just flew away, like a small and silent bird.

When he did research on Google he found out that limerence was very old. It went back to the Romans. It went back to the Greeks. It probably went back to the cavemen.

The important thing now was the something that became an everything that had a name and it was not Louise.

It had never been love. It was limerence.

If you doubt this story or are curious about it, look it up yourself.

Limerence.

There was a glowing and nuclear power in the word, a very ancient thing that is written on our bones. That was what Larry realized. There is power in a story made of words and language.

The author would like you to know that you can use just such a word, such a story as this one, to survive.

The Man Who Made Whirligigs

He was Whimsy999. She was Vivacious002. He was seeking a woman. She was seeking a man. He was looking for fun. She was looking for a good time. They both thought, in the long term, it might be good to "find real love." Oh, and he made whirligigs.

"Really," Vivacious wrote, "whirligigs?"

"Really," wrote Whimsy. "And wind chimes. I make lots of those, they're popular." He made his living by going to trade shows, setting up his little kiosk-tent at outdoor music festivals in the summer. He followed a festival circuit, he told her, which meant he had winters pretty much off. "That is when I make new designs, I do my creative stuff."

He also made mobiles, blue and gold and some the color of sunrise over the Rocky Mountains. "I like to make things that move," he said. "I like motion."

Vivacious tried to decide if that was a sexual innuendo. If he was getting at something.

They decided to meet at a farmers' market in Corrales, New Mexico, on a Wednesday afternoon, during the International Balloon Fiesta. "I hear they have nice soup," said Whimsy. "Corn chowder and such."

"I like that," said Vivacious, who wasn't feeling really sure about meeting for soup at a farmers' market, but what the hey?

"I'll be the guy wearing the earring. And the scarf."

"A scarf?" asked Vivacious. *An earring*, she thought. She was beginning to feel funny about this.

"Yes," he said, "blue. By the way, my name is Al."

Al. She liked "Whimsy" so much better than "Al." In fact, she wasn't really sure about going to eat chowder at a farmers' market with a guy named Al who wore an earring and a blue scarf, a man who made whirligigs, especially during the International Balloon Fiesta, a time when the town was crawling with available men. And she wasn't even really sure what a whirligig was. Something that swirls and moves and makes shadows, she thought. She might have seen one once in a movie. Or at her aunt Tania's farm. Her aunt Tania was into things like that. In fact, maybe she should introduce this Al to Aunt Tania. They might have more in common.

Al was Jewish and made much of it, using Yiddish words and such. "I make all this *mishegas*, and people, they love it," he said.

Vivacious was Latina and made much of it. She pronounced it *Lateeeena*. When she wasn't being Vivacious, she was called Blanquita. She cooked a rocking chili con carne and made huevos rancheros on the weekends for her two sisters and their mother, who all shared a condo in Albuquerque's Northeast Heights. She worked as a hairdresser at A La Beauté. She wasn't really sure what that translated to, or quite what language it was, but she thought it might be French, or Italian. Her boss was Rico, a transvestite Puerto Rican (hence "Rico"), who liked to use French-ish words whenever possible, like "croissant," which he pronounced *cwaaasohn*. Blanquita wasn't sure if it was a real aspiration to speak French or a gay thing, so she just tried to steer clear of it, to keep on the safe side. She wanted to keep her job. It was the third salon she had worked for in the past six months. She'd been fired from one because her clients complained about her smoking. "Who wants to be touched with tobacco hands?" said one old blue-hair who came in for the same do every week, what she and her fellow dressers called the "high and dry." (Reference to the fact that these women wanted their hair teased up high to cover the thinning and sometimes bald spots beneath. And they were willing to sit under a hot dryer for half an hour to achieve this effect.) The woman's name was Lucille and she demanded that Hot Cuts fire Blanquita or she and all her friends would decamp down the street to Le Boutique Rose.

After that, Vivacious, aka Blanquita, quit smoking but was fired from her next job for the smacking noise she made while chewing the nicotine gum that had helped her quit.

Rico, at A La Beauté, had a very strong jawline and smelled of Chanel No. 5. She knew this because she had once bought a bottle and still had it, in her closet, for a special occasion that had yet to arrive. The idea of the perfume tucked in the closet reminded her of the way spring could be tucked underneath winter snow, waiting to bloom. Rico, on the other hand, wasn't waiting. He was a closet intellectual, reading the existentialists, especially Sartre and Camus, in between customers. He wore Chanel No. 5 every day. And that stuff was expensive.

When Rico hired Blanquita he did so with a warning: "You watch your customers, you act nice and you give them a nice look, Blanquita, sweetie. And I give you a beeg raise. Okay, sweetie? You give me problemas and *sayonara*. Okay, sweetie? *Me entiendes?* Si vu play?"

She did. *Entender*, that is.

Al was in Albuquerque for the International Balloon Fiesta and had searched online for "single hotties" to keep him company, which is how he came upon Vivacious. He had been to the festival every year for the past twenty years and found it a very good venue for selling his wares. But he had another reason for being there this year, one he had not told anyone about, not a soul.

It was a hot and dusty day, and already the haze was setting in. Air pollution in Albuquerque tended to get trapped in the bowl of the Rio Grande valley like a gray and toxic soup. The balloons suspended over the haze looked odd and festive. In contrast to the gray and putrid air they seemed out of place, overly bright. Everywhere, people were peeling off jackets and pointing up at the sky. Pretty, pretty inflatable things! Large and bright. Some were in shapes like a teapot and a phone book that said "Yellow Pages." Over the years more and more of the balloons seemed to be advertisements. There was a giant bottle of Tabasco sauce balloon. There was a globe balloon. There was a Nike sneaker balloon and several basketballs. There was a carton of milk from a local dairy.

Vivacious looked across the farmers' market for a man in a blue scarf, with an earring. A man who might be called "Al." What the heck was she doing anyway? How desperate does a girl get? "Ah, Jewish, so he has some *dinero*, does this one?" teased her sister Madelena. Madelena was studying at TVI—the Technical Vocational Institute—for her electrician's license, after which she thought she might get a degree in engineering at UNM. After that she would go and work for Intel on the West Mesa in Albuquerque. Then she would get a house up there and a nice car (Volvo station wagons actually *called* to her) and marry an engineer. She would like a daughter named Violeta and a son named Miguel. She could call him Miguelito.

"Um, do you think you might be, like, getting ahead of yourself a little?" Blanquita would ask when Madelena would rhapsodize about her possible future.

"Just because some of us have dreams, Blanquita, and aren't settling for some lame hairdressing career."

"It's not lame, I go to workshops!" Blanquita said. But now that she stood in the farmers' market in the sultry and somewhat unbreathable air, in the rotund shadows of passing balloons like a festival of bright clouds, looking for some guy she met online, she did have to admit—this was hardly a life. Okay, it was lame. Just then a man stepped up behind her.

"Hey there, gorgeous. You must be Vivacious," the man said.

"How did you know?" she asked, checking the man out. He was about five feet four inches and had a beard. And, yes, an earring and a blue scarf tied over his head behind his ears, like a gypsy. *Probably bald under there*, she thought. Bald guys always wore baseball hats and scarf things and stuff. It was as if covering it up made it cool to be losing hair. She preferred it when they just shaved their heads. A bald head could be sexy, even. Look at all those pro basketball players.

"The way you are looking," Al said. "Like you don't know quite who you are looking for. So, wanna have some lunch?"

This was the problem with the online thing. You meet someone and they are mysterious, they are cool and funny and cloaked behind a screen. In the real world they are short and hide their baldness. "Sure," she said, wishing she could just go home.

They drove in his little RV to a park and sat under a tree at a picnic table and Al bought them each a burrito. Nearby a checkered balloon sailed above the tree line. People pointed and stared, like it was a rare bird or a lunar eclipse. Blanquita smiled. "Seen one balloon fiesta, seen 'em all," she said.

Al nodded. He sort of liked her jaded attitude, this Vivacious. It was sexy.

"So, you like to swim?" he asked. His motel had a pool. "I live in the RV almost all year, so when I can I get a hotel room," he said, with a wink.

Here we go with the motel, she thought. But the day was getting hotter and the idea of floating in warm chlorine-laden water was somewhat appealing just then. It was her day off and she didn't want to spend it home with her sisters and mother, who could get on her nerves. "I do, we could," she said.

So they finished up their burritos, she picked up a suit Walmart, and they headed to the Days Inn. Al's RV was full of boxes and cartons packed with stuff. On the floor a few things were laid out, as if he had been working on them. He picked up a whirligig and it immediately began to twirl, like a little wooden tornado.

"So that," she said, "is a whirligig. I was trying to remember." He held up another one and it twirled as well. It was inlaid with bits of glass and colored beads. She drew a breath. "It is so beautiful," she said. "I *like* that one."

"Then it is yours," said Al. She had nice eyes and generous thighs he could imagine touching, like soft pillows. He would like to sink into her, a feather bed of a woman.

They swam in the pool and then had drinks with the chase team for the Tabasco sauce balloon, who were also staying at the Days Inn, two guys named Steve and Jerry. They invited Al and Blanquita to go up in the balloon. "It's fun. It's not at all scary," said Steve. "It's like being a cloud, very peaceful."

"I have never wanted to be a cloud," laughed Blanquita. "And I hate heights. But thanks, that's sweet."

In the morning Al's cell phone rang. There beside him was Blanquita, snoring softly. They had drunk wine spritzers and swam in the hotel pool until midnight.

Al gave Blanquita a little shake, brushing her hair out of her face. She looked older in the morning light but still very beautiful and very exotic. He liked the way she said "Al," like *all*. She tasted of something oddly sweet. He had realized it was the nicotine gum. It had a chemical sweetness that was not unpleasant. He liked it. He had to wake her because of the important thing he had to do. He had an appointment at noon.

She waved him away. She would sleep in.

He walked over to the window and pulled back the curtains to reveal the sky already gray with hot smog.

His heart started up a little. He had not told anyone about this day. And here he was with this woman on it. It was possibly the most important day of his life. He had spent a day selling his wares in his tent at the fiesta grounds, which meant that it must be the fifth. He looked at his watch. It was. The fifth. He had an appointment with the social workers. He had had six interviews, and had gone through all sorts of screenings. They had done background check after background check. And then he had gone online and hooked up with this . . . Blanquita. What was he thinking?

"Vivacious," said Al, "Blanquita!"

"What?" she said, peering out from beneath the pillow, looking annoyed. "I don't wanna go up in a balloon. I am afraid of heights."

"No, it's just that I have to leave. I have to go to Gallup."

"Gallup?" she said. Nobody went to Gallup. It was the last stop before Arizona on Route 66, a strip of bars and drunken Navajo people with their government checks, wannabe artists who couldn't afford Santa Fe, and a lot of Middle Eastern jewelry dealers who made a lot of people feel just plain suspicious ever since 9-11.

"Yes," said Al, suddenly feeling warmly toward her. "I have to go. Now. If you wanna come, you can, but I have to leave."

"Can we at least get some breakfast?" she asked.

"Sure," he said.

Blanquita sat up. She had not expected this little odd man who had made love to her so passionately all night to be so mysterious. "Really? Gallup?"

Al had told nobody about Betty. Not even his own mother, and here he was about to tell a stranger. Vivacious, the Internet vixen. In some odd way it seemed appropriate, to tell this Internet-found hoochie about his Internet-found daughter-to-be. He smiled.

They drove fast. It was already a quarter to nine and it would be bad form to be late. They went over a long stretch of low hills and then they passed Acoma Pueblo, "the so-called Sky City," Al said.

"Yes," said Blanquita, "they lived up on that mesa. A long time ago, they got sick of the Spanish priests telling them what to do and all, so they rounded 'em up and pushed them off the edge. Like pirates would. Off the plank, you know."

This chick has some spunk, Al thought. And he admitted it, he liked that. They drove over the rim of a red canyon that looked chopped open, a piece of exposed meat.

Above them a blue and green Tabasco-sauce-shaped balloon floated. "It's them," said Blanquita, pointing up. It was, the guys they had drunk stingers and wine coolers with the night before. They waved down, arms like teensy sticks. They looked like insects. "It's Steve and Jerry."

"Wow," said Al, "it is!" The colorful balloon looked so bright over the badlands. Long ago, a volcano had spit up all over the place, left a dark spew of black rock that seemed crumbled, a giant package of broken Oreos sprinkled over the hills.

"So where are we going?" asked Blanquita, aka Vivacious.

"To meet the social workers," he said. "And get my daughter." He paused. "I am adopting!"

Her name was Betty and she had been born to a Navajo couple who had been killed in a terrible car accident the previous summer. Their four children had all been absorbed into the homes of extended family. But Betty was a special-needs child, and nobody felt equipped to take her in. Nobody except Al. He had decided the previous winter he wanted a daughter. He was fifty-six years old and was giving up on the perfect Jewish woman thing. He just wanted a child to love and to raise; he had chosen Betty off a website for special-needs adoptions. She was tiny and "slow" and had a harelip. She had "trouble learning." But she was "pleasant and sweet" and "liked cats," the website said. Al had a cat and loved children. He liked the way they could smell of dust and melted candy. The way their hands got sticky so easily and they laughed with such abandon. He had begun to feel he would never hear that sound in his own life. He had begun to feel very saddened by that. So he was adopting. He was adopting Betty.

He was sure his family would be discouraging. His mother, especially. She had disapproved of all his girl-friends, one right after another, for thirty years. Nobody good enough for her boychik. A little Navajo girl? It would certainly give Esther the famous "agita" which she had suffered for over twenty years—so he would just hold off on sharing the news, until Rosh Hashanah at least, when he would be home in New York and she would find out. That would give him several months to get used to little Betty and for Betty to get used to him. They would travel around in his RV selling the famous whirligigs. He would homeschool her. They would be happy, little Betty and he. He would not judge her for her harelip and slowness, and she, in turn, would love him for taking her in and for his marvelous and beautiful whirligigs, mobiles, and chimes. That was how he pictured it, anyway.

But now, here he was, a man with an Internet hoochie woman in tow. He could hardly leave Blanquita alone in the RV; that would be rude. But he could hardly bring her, either. They would wonder, of course, who she was. Or maybe they would like it, the appearance of a woman. A potential mother for this girl, they might even think. It could, actually, be helpful. He knew they still had misgivings about him.

"And now is when you get her? Today? In Gallup?"

"Yes," he said to Blanquita. "I know it seems weird, but I have been planning this for a long time."

They had to stop in Grants to fill up the RV; the thing guzzled fuel like a drunk. It felt good to rise up out of the Rio Grande valley and gain a little altitude, get away from the smoggy hot city. They drove past the Continental Divide and to a place where a deep mesa abutted a canyon and a distant rainstorm wagged like a gray finger, scolding down from the sky. Then they came to the Giant Truck Stop. It was a mall of a truck stop. Right there in the middle of seeming nowhere. They stopped for some breakfast. Al had grits and steak; Blanquita had red chili stew. "I make it better," she said.

He smiled. He was nervous. Soon he would meet Betty. That was when he got the idea. He would ask Blanquita to wait right there, at the truck stop. "I will come right back and get you," he said. "I just need to make a good impression. You know."

"And I would make it a bad impression?" Blanquita asked.

"Well, we are just new friends and all and this is serious business. I am adopting a little girl today."

"Just why are you doing this, anyway?" Blanquita asked. "Do you think you can handle it? It's a lot of work, you know."

"Of course I know," Al said. He was feeling annoyed. He had been planning this day for over two years.

"Okay," said Blanquita, "I'll wait here. Just because I know they aren't expecting me or anything, not that there is anything *wrong* with me."

"Oh, no!" said Al, "of course not, you're great! I just didn't tell them about . . . you know . . . any kind of partner. They do a lot of background checking, in advance." He wiped his mouth hard, with a napkin, like he was wiping a dead bug off a window.

"Okay, then," said Blanquita, glancing around the Giant Truck Stop. There a little shop she could browse in, a place with magazines. And she could always have coffee and read the paper. "So, like, when will you be back?"

"Oh, not long . . . very soon, in fact."

"Okay," said Blanquita. She leaned over and gave Al a little kiss. "That is for last night. For being so sweet and all."

"My pleasure," he said, and winked at her.

It was afternoon. He was right on time. Al straightened his collar and tucked in his shirt. He had brought the adoption papers his lawyer had drawn up. *Here goes*, he thought. He was expecting . . . what was he expecting? He was expecting a little girl, a child to love.

They were meeting at the Office of Family Affairs and Planning, a typical government office, yellow painted cinder block walls, linoleum floors. Smelled of Mr. Clean. He had driven through the town fast, past a motel that looked like concrete teepees, and another with a cowboy lassoing a calf. Gallup was famous for its neon signs. He had seen a book about it.

There, sitting on a bench with a blue dress on, between the two social workers, was the girl. She looked down at her shoes. She was tiny. Much smaller than he had imagined. She was wearing a shirt that said "I heart Rodeo."

He shook the hand of the first social worker. "Al," he said.

"Mark," said the man. "And this is . . ."

"Betty?" he said, completing the sentence.

The girl looked up for the first time. He saw her and she saw him. Her face was full of trepidation. Beside her was a suitcase and a bag of stuffed animals.

"Are those your friends?" asked Al.

Betty nodded. He pulled over a chair and sat across from them.

"What are their names?"

She looked down at her shoes again.

"Betty is a little shy, but I am sure she will come around."

"That one looks like it should be named Jimmy," Al said, pointing to a stuffed dolphin.

"It's a girl," whispered Betty. "Her name is Darlene."

"Of course, I should have known it is a girl. She is so pretty."

The social workers went over the paperwork, and then they all went out for an early supper at Earl's restaurant. It was a diner-ish place, very local, with people walking from one table to the next to say hello to one another. A few people stared over at Al and the social workers; he could tell they were wondering what these white people were doing with the little Navajo girl. He smiled to himself. He was imagining a time someday when he and Betty would hike the Grand Canyon or he would watch her play the violin in a school concert.

What the other people were thinking was *Perv white guy, staring at that little girl.* And he could feel it, their distrust, their judgmental thoughts. They were like heat-seeking missile thoughts; they pierced his warm skin and moved down toward his even warmer heart. But right there he stopped them. Al who made whirligigs reflected on what he knew for sure about himself: He was a good man. He had a simple craft. He wanted a family. He might even adopt a boy as well, who knows? He was not a person who would ever hurt anyone.

Just then, as he thought that thought, as he was commending himself on his inner goodness, he remembered her: Blanquita. And he knew he had left her sitting at the Giant Truck Stop, waiting for him. He flushed red with the recognition of it. That he had everything in life he needed now. As he looked at Betty his heart swelled. He could help her with her math. He could buy her stuffed animals for Christmas. He could . . . he could do so many things for her, he could hardly wait to begin. He would be her father.

When they reached the RV, having signed off on all the paperwork, the social workers told Al he had passed the psychological exam with flying colors and muster of every sort. He was *a dad*. They all shook hands and smiled. What a good deed was being done. What fortune that Al wanted Betty and Betty needed Al.

But Betty looked terrified as the social workers drove away. She was visibly shaking. Looking at her tremble, Al felt for the first time the huge and real weight of this decision, this responsibility. She was a person. And his heart went out to her. He could imagine her fear.

"Here," he said. "Look at this . . ." He held up a wooden whirligig in the breeze. To his delight, she smiled. She reached out her hand to touch the spinning top of wood. Her smile broadened and it became a laugh. Not a big one, not a guffaw, or even a chuckle. But yes, a definite laugh. Inside the laugh Al thought he could hear the echo of a deep and resonant intelligence, a certain beauty. His heart bloomed.

It was getting dark and they began to drive. Al had strapped Betty into a car seat. She was very small for her age. He turned onto the main road of Gallup and then drove down onto the interstate. His foot pressed on the gas, and it occurred to him he was going to do what might be considered a very bad thing. He would not stop at the Giant Truck Stop. He would not go and get Blanquita. He would not drive back to Albuquerque. In fact, he would not do anything he had ever done before. Al, aka Whimsy999, a man who made whirligigs, was a father now, and nothing else mattered.

Heart Food

Every evening, after her daughter, Lillypie, had been bathed, pajamed, watered, told a long story about forest fairies, and put to bed in her room on the second floor of their house, Ophelia retreated downstairs. A single mother, exhausted from a long day of work and child care, she would make herself a cup of stiff tea—oolong or a chai concoction with elongated strands of honey that would sink into the dark liquid and pool at the bottom in a deep reservoir of sweet. She would dim the lights and close the curtains, shutting out the night, and put on music from one of the easy-listening channels on her television—either the new age channel or the light jazz station—and sit herself on the couch to unravel the stress of the day. She would sip the tea and then begin her list of affirmations:

You are a good person.
You try your best every day.

You accept you have made mistakes.
You deserve love.

Then, having restored her ego to some semblance of peace, she would sit herself cross-legged, in a meditation position, with her ankles folded over her thighs, and proceed to unlatch her chest, swing open the little door there, reach in and take out her heart from her rib cage.

It was blue-red and purpled with veins, a normal heart by anyone's standards, yet a heart in need of attention—she could tell by the way it looked up at her, so gratefully, after she released it. It gazed into her eyes with a sense of longing, a gentle question always on its face, which she took to mean *What now, my dear?*

In the quiet of the living room with the washing machine chugging away in an adjacent room, the refrigerator humming in the kitchen, a gentle *ommm*, the creak and rattle of the house all around in the wind and weather outside, the cats sleeping in their baskets, the dog in his corner, having been given his quota of attention for the day, she finally had time and space to speak with her heart.

Sometimes she told her heart a story the way she told her daughter stories. Sometimes she just sat there and stroked it gently, or rubbed it around the top, in the small spot between where her aorta and coronary arteries were set, a place she liked to think of as between its ears. Her heart loved this and after a few seconds, inevitably, it would begin to purr. *I love you, heart,* she would say. *You know I do.*

She knew her heart had been through a lot. That time in Panama, for example, when she was very young and working for the Peace Corps. A local fisherman had facilitated the exchange of romantic little notes between her and an anthropologist on the mainland for months, only for her to be told she was not the *one,* that night in Boca del Toro, when he came across from Chiriqui Grande in the fishing boat. On his one visit to the island, they had made love for hours, after which he whispered to her softly, not that he loved her but that he would not be back. It was love but not *the* love, he said.

Then there was the time she went all the way to Anchorage to see the man from graduate school who had taken a teaching job there. He had written her weekly, and so terribly sweetly, for seven years, culminating in an invitation to visit that made her heart so hopeful, so pumped with the adrenaline elixir of affection, she felt it would ignite from the warmth. She had arrived to find he had a family of six, a new baby in the arms of his second wife. "I never dreamed you would actually come," he had said. "I am so, so sorry."

But, most serious of all, her heart had weathered the foibles of her husband, Rick, he of the somber, nuanced paintings of little villages set among hills, the woman doing a rope trick, the woman balancing a planet on her head, the woman on fire. What love, what passion was inscribed in those paintings. Love of color, color of love, love of light, light of love, love of her own aspect and appearance, which appeared in so many of them. Sadly, her husband told lies the way other people ordered Chinese food—he'd memorized the entire menu of untruths and partook thereof with a certain regularity and purpose. It was as if he felt it was his constitutional right to lie, listed in the Bill of Rights of his body. It was his tongue, after all, his vocal cords, his mouth. Does not one have the right to use one's own organs any way one pleases, seeing that they belong to oneself?

Her heart had taken that particularly hard. It told her husband's vocal cords that they were unethical and insensitive, and would carry a stain from this. Her heart was very proud of the fact that it did not, ever, lie. Just as it was its job to filter out the soiled blood from the sweet every minute of every day, it was the heart's job to stick with verity.

Her heart took this truth job oh so seriously and thought that the vocal cords, the mouth, and the tongue of the husband should take their jobs seriously as well.

"Sorry," said the man's mouth. "It wasn't meant to hurt her."

Her heart had survived these things. But Ophelia knew she owed her heart something for all this wear and tear. A favor. She had thought up a number of things to do for her heart over the years, to make it feel safe, and better. For example, when it was feeling very upset, pounding out a drumroll of angst, she would sometimes lay her heart down on the pillow beside Lillypie, sleeping, for a while, and that seemed to calm it immensely. Lillypie still sucked her thumb; she had the habit of lisping out the smallest yet most momentous things in her sleep between the sucking sounds. Like "Right here, bunny, next to me," and "These dandelions are my friends."

The heart loved that, to lie beside Lillypie and listen to the sentences. And loved it most when Lillypie would laugh, with abandon, as she slept. While the heart didn't know exactly what Lillypie was laughing about, it didn't care. That laughter was the heart's food. A heart vitamin infusion. No matter what had happened during the day, Lillypie's laughter soothed it, calmed it down and made it whole again. The ventricles squeezed open and shut in response. The left atrium and right atrium strummed in pleasure. Her heart whispered, "I love you so much," to her daughter's ears and her daughter's ears smiled. "Love you back," they said. And all was well then. Or better, anyway.

This was one way she had kept her heart happy for years. Yet there were people who frowned on this behavior. "One shouldn't let one's heart sleep next to one's child," they said. After a certain age, it was considered a bad idea. Lillypie was now six, too old, they said, to be lying next to an open, beating heart at night. No matter what that heart needed, the child's needs were more im-portant, and she needed to sleep and sleep alone.

"But it doesn't wake her," Ophelia protested. "She doesn't even know it's there."

"Doesn't matter," said these self-appointed experts (and most everyone had an opinion about the heart, wherever she went).

So, in time, she had stopped laying her heart next to Lillypie and had taken up other things to soothe it.

A more recent tactic was to take her heart with her to the computer, flick it on so its blue gaze would blink open, like a wide and square eye. Then she would go online to find friends for her heart.

At first her heart protested. "Not real," it said. "C'mon!"

In time, however, her heart had grown to see the value. There were folks to meet, love to be had, though it was a very muffled love, mediated as it was through the screen and the keyboard upon which Ophelia typed.

On one particular lonely night, after Lillypie was asleep in her bed, watered and storied and tucked in, Ophelia took her uncaged heart to her computer and typed in the URL of Catchahubby.com. Faces bloomed; descriptions of the owners' own lonely, lonely hearts bloomed across the screen. Her little heart fluttered, its mitral valve gasped, and then, did it giggle? She touched it softly, between the ears. She typed in words to one person in particular, a man with sad sad eyes.

"Greetings," the man typed.

"Hi," she typed back.

The man was sad, he said, because his own daughter had rejected him, forced by his ex-wife to choose. Ophelia's heart sighed in her lap. As the conversation progressed, she could feel it shuddering. And then, as the man described his situation, all alone, with neither wife nor child, her heart began softly to weep.

This is too sad, said her heart. Try someone else.

A man appeared on her screen with a hungry look.

"Hello there," he typed. "Whatcha doin'?"

Tell him we are just sitting here, wondering where love is.

"Just here," she typed.

"You are gorgeous," the man typed.

"You 2," she typed.

"Skype?" asked the man.

She turned on her computer's camera. There was the man, his hairy undressed chest shockingly visible. His mouth agape.

"Down on all fours," he commanded.

X out, *x* out, her heart screamed. She did, but for the two of them the chesty man lingered, like an afterimage in the air, for some time. His brutish face a slash across the night.

Then Ophelia found another man, a man who lived nearby. He typed that he liked her face. He had a daughter, as she did, asleep in another room. He asked what her favorite color was.

This is more like it, the heart said.

"Purple," she replied.

"Me too," he typed. "Me too! What do you do?"

"I work for an insurance company," Ophelia typed. "You?"

"I make things," he typed back.

"Skype?" she typed.

She was a bit afraid to Skype after the brutish-man incident, but she tentatively turned on her camera. A beautiful man stood there, holding a beautiful kite. It was purple, with orange wings, like a jungle bird.

"Beautiful," she said.

"So you like it?"

"I do," she answered.

"I made it."

Ask him where he flies such a kite, said her heart.

"I fly it on the beach, you should come. I have many!"

Her heart smiled.

"Sounds fun," she said.

On the weekends Ophelia would take her daughter to ballet. Lillypie was going to be in a recital and she would be gone all morning, practicing pirouettes and sashays and relevés. In the recital she was to be a squirrel.

"I don't want to be a squirrel," she confided in her mother over a grilled cheese sandwich with pickles at a diner, their after-ballet tradition. "I want to be one of the forest fairies."

"Fairies are fun but squirrels get to jump, they get to spin."

"I still want to be a fairy," she said. "Fairies can spin."

"I know, love," Ophelia said. "I will ask and see if we can make you a fairy."

"Thank you, Momma," Lillypie said, her eyes filling with gratitude.

After dropping off Lillypie at her class, Ophelia drove to the beach and met the man who made things, the man with the kites. He was standing right there on the beach, in the wind, and the kite was right next to him, straining on its string, a playful bird on a leash. When he saw her, his eyes bloomed and he let the kite leap. It jumped into the wind and did a little orange and purple dance there. She thought of Lillypie, and how much she would love the bright bird kite, and how she might like the man with the kite.

"Here," he said, and handed her the spool of string. Their fingers touched. The kite pounced out of his hand into hers and she could feel it pulling toward the sun. It was as if he had handed her an enthusiastic living thing.

It was a windy day, a bright day; the kite made a loud flapping sound. They barely spoke, these two, just took turns unspooling the kite into the sky, and watching it. They laughed, and ran, and he chased her as she bolted down the beach and when he caught her he placed his hands on her hips, holding Ophelia as she held the kite. In her chest her heart nodded.

When she went to retrieve Lillypie, she asked the ballet teacher if there was any way at all that Lillypie could be a fairy. "She is going through a hard time," Ophelia said.

"I know, she told me," the ballet teacher said. "Her father is far away and she isn't sure if he will return?"

"Something like that," Ophelia said.

"I will see what I can do," the teacher said.

That night when she tucked in Lillypie, Lillypie asked, "Momma, do I get to be a fairy?"

"We are seeing what can be done."

"Oh, thank you, Momma, thank you!"

"Don't thank me yet," Ophelia said.

After Lillypie fell asleep, Ophelia went downstairs and made her tea. She sat on the couch cross-legged with her feet tucked upon her thighs. *You are a good person,* she chanted to herself.

You try your best every day.
You accept you have made mistakes.
You deserve love.

Then she unlatched and opened the little door to her chest. Her heart practically flew out. Kite man! Kite man! it said.

I know, she said.

She flipped on the computer to look for him but he wasn't there. In his place was a host of unfamiliar faces, each one with a full load of sorrow and loneliness.

Where is he? her heart asked, with a sigh.

No idea, she said.

Try to find him!

Ophelia did a search on "Kite," "maker," and the name of her town.

Nothing. She realized that, clearly undergoing some bout of temporary insanity, she had never even asked the man his name.

That wasn't smart, said her heart.

Don't get snippy, she said.

She went back to the couch and was about to replace the heart in its cage when her heart said, Not yet. We aren't done. We need to find the kite man.

What do you want from me? she asked.

More than this. In her hands her heart was shaking.

I am sorry, she said. I am sorry, heart.

Her heart looked up at her. Are you? it asked. Really?

Then take me upstairs, let me lie beside Lillypie and hear her laugh in her sleep.

Heart, you know she is too old for that now.

Please, begged her heart. Please.

Ophelia could see that her heart would have its way, so she cupped it in her hands as she begrudgingly mounted the stairs and then quietly entered Lillypie's room. Her daughter was sleeping so deeply, her head indenting the pillow, tiny snores emitting from her nose, the sucking sound of her mouth around her thumb, a menagerie of stuffed animals all around her. Ophelia carefully placed her heart on the pillow beside her.

Her heart settled in and sighed. It breathed in the smell of little girl, a compilation of dust, popsicle sweat, and Love's Baby Soft shampoo. It was the smell of dreams and hope. It also had a vague scent of sadness. "Just make me a fairy," Lillypie suddenly said, from the midst of her dream.

The heart listened.

The heart was sad also; it knew there was little chance of finding the kite man. It knew that love had slipped away, just like a kite on the wind that had escaped its string. The heart was sure of only one thing, one thing in the world: Lillypie, the smell of her, her solid body, her own fledgling beautiful heart, one foot splayed off the edge of the bed, her small hands tucked beneath her head.

You will be a fairy, her heart whispered to Lillypie's dream.

Thank you, the dream said.

You are welcome, said the heart, closing its eyes. You can take me back now, it said to Ophelia. Put me in my cage. And for a while, I think I would like to just stay there.

I understand, said Ophelia. And for a long time after that, she left her heart there inside her chest. She did not go on the computer and type words to the universe of lonely men. She just lived her life, day to day.

And it was okay. Lillypie did get to be a fairy after all, and an ecstatic, leaping, twirling fairy she was. She was the best of the fairy pack, it was obvious to everyone.

Dog People

C larissa was in the park with her dog when a man stepped up to her, quite unexpectedly.

"What is his or her name?" the man asked.

It took Clarissa a moment to register the question—she was taken aback by the man himself, his blue eyes reminding her suddenly of those early pictures of the earth, taken from the moon.

"Zeus," she said; "it's a he. I mean a boy."

"Beautiful dog," said the man. His own dog loitered nearby, a scrappy thing, with a patch of fur missing from one side, like a worn-out rug. One could hardly reply with a compliment about this man's dog's beauty. A pause followed that was uncomfortably long, until Clarissa filled it by asking the man's dog's name.

"You won't believe it if I tell you," the man said.

"Try me," said Clarissa.

"Juno," said the man. "It's a she."

They laughed a bit, each one thinking how odd and strange it was to meet another person who had a dog named after a deity of antiquity, not to mention that these two deities were married to each other. Each had met many people online with whom they had experienced coincidences, but somehow in the real world such things seemed, well, realer, and coincidences more coincidental.

"Live around here?" the man asked.

"Just down the street," said Clarissa. "How about you?"

"Oh I live a bit a ways, actually," he said. "In a beautiful place in the mountains. By the way, I'm Harry."

"Clarissa."

"Good to meetcha," he said. "I come here on Tuesdays, in the mornings, and walk my dog here. I have a business deal in the neighborhood."

"I see," said Clarissa, thinking how odd it was he should tell her his dog walking schedule, unless, of course, he meant to provide her an easy way to see him again. "We come here all the time, this is our main park," she said, giving him a way back.

"Cool," said the man named Harry.

"I met a man," Clarissa told her friend Molly, later in the day, in an instant message on Facebook.

"E-clectic, Catch, or PCF?" her friend asked. Lots of people met on Pretty Cool Fish, but it was also wellknown as a place for the desperate. It was free to join and a sort of last resort for women of a certain age, like around forty-two, which happened to be the age of both Molly and Clarissa. If a woman met a person on PCF she often wanted to hide that fact, and would say it happened on Catch or E-clectic.

"I met him at the park, walking Zeus," Clarissa said.

"Oh wow," Molly wrote back. "A real-world man. You don't hear much about that anymore."

"No," Clarissa agreed. "You don't."

They stopped typing for a moment, each one thinking about what the implications of real-world men might be.

"Flesh and bone could have some pluses," Molly said, "like none of that awful confusion in e-mails, not getting the tone right."

"True, and no chance he would just vanish one day from your inbox. Like if he met someone else and just poof!"

"Been there, done that," Molly said, "bought the tee shirt. And don't you love how sometimes they just write you and say 'done'?"

"Or vanish and then come back six months later like it is no big deal they just blew you off."

"The rudeness factor, it's just expected!"

Next Tuesday: park, dog run, same time, he was there. "Hey, Clarissa," the man waved, from across the dog run, where Juno was sniffing the butt of a chubby Dalmatian.

"Hey there," she said, feeling a little soft-shoe routine of anticipation tap up in her chest.

Harry, the real man, walked over, and she had a chance to get a sense of the whole person of him. He was medium height and build and had a goatee. He looked to be fortysomething, or maybe a bit older.

"So how's Juno?" she asked.

"Oh, she is fine, but a little lonely these days, I think. How is Zeus?"

His dog, Juno, was lonely? How could one tell when one's dog was lonely, anyway? What did the real man Harry mean by that? Was this a thinly veiled way of talking about himself? Was she supposed to say that Zeus was lonely, too?

"He's great. Chased a squirrel up a tree and is feeling very proud of himself for it, I think."

The real man Harry cut to the chase: "I live about twenty miles away, in the woods; it's a great place for dogs to run and play free," he said. "You and Zeus should come out sometime, it would be fun."

What? This was incredibly sudden and direct. At that moment she was somewhat embarrassed to notice that Zeus was sniffing Juno's behind rather blatantly. Was Harry the real man asking her out after two chance encounters in the park? After months of trolling for men online it seemed ironic, to say the least, that a real man should trip into her life so easily.

"Sounds cool," she said, not wanting to seem too eager or desperate, but there was also the danger factor to consider. Real man Harry might be a serial killer, luring her to his den of torture and real peril. She had heard that serial killers sometimes used cute pets as bait. But Juno was really not that cute and real man Harry seemed very sincere. She took the note on which he scribbled his number and e-mail and address. "It's easy to find," he said. "We are always around, except on Tuesday mornings, when I have a little business in town."

"What sort of business?" Clarissa asked, curiously.

"Real estate. I am selling off some property," he said.

"I see," Clarissa said.

Later, on Facebook chat, she told Molly all about it. "A beard, what kind of beard? Molly said. "Please say it isn't a ZZ Top kind of thing!"

Clarissa wrote back: "Oh, no, something small and neat."

"Oh, please say a soul patch, those are so cute."

"Nope. A beard. Like a goatee thing."

"Oh, a goatee, like Rasputin."

"Well, yes," Clarissa wrote back. "I guess it is a little Rasputinish."

"Watch out for those Rasputin-bearded men!" Molly wrote.

"OK then, I will, c-ya," Clarissa wrote. She got annoyed with Molly sometimes, how she always riffed on everything in a negative way. She had been feeling fairly nice about Harry the real man and did not like this suggestion—or her own nagging suspicion—that he might be a weirdo.

Two days later she wrote an e-mail to Harry, but then she erased it. It was weird to e-mail a man you really didn't know. But then, she did that all the time with men she met on Catch and PCF. That was funny. To e-mail a real-world man was odd, but a man in the ether, acceptable.

Note to self, Clarissa thought: *Temper fears of real-world men. Do not be prejudiced against them for having three dimensions.*

The next Tuesday when she was walking Zeus, Harry was there again. He walked right over. "Today is my last day here with Juno," he said. "I sold my property this morning!"

"Mazel tov!" she said. "I think—that's a good thing, right?"

"It is!" he said. "But it's a bad thing, because now Juno and I will no longer have opportunities to run into you and Zeus."

"Awwww," said Clarissa. "That's sweet." She blushed.

"You probably never wrote or called because it seemed too weird, calling out to a stranger, basically."

"Yeah, it did," she said, blushing again.

"You are blushing," said Harry.

"I am?" Clarissa asked.

"Either that or you have developed a very bad and sudden sunburn."

"You're funny," Clarissa said.

"I am," said Harry, as if realizing for the first time that he might be.

They laughed. After chatting a few more minutes Clarissa gave Harry her e-mail. Later that afternoon he wrote her.

"This is a picture of my land," he wrote. "On top of Sayer's Point, and has four peaks and two streams, as well as a small pond. I also have a smaller house where I live down the road. There are lots of fun things to do there."

"Wowwee," Clarissa typed back.

"So would you like to visit sometime?"

"Sure."

"How about Saturday?"

The real-world man was relentless. The date was set. Still, Clarissa had a funny feeling about it. Real world Harry seemed almost too real, too eager. When he had brushed against her hand when they were parting, it left her feeling lightly zapped, like she had accidently touched a wrong part of the toaster.

That Saturday, driving to Harry's house in the mountains with her dog, Zeus, in the back of her car, Clarissa felt very alert and unsure. Was this a good idea even, driving to meet a man at his house, a man she barely knew? Yet she also felt great anticipation, and that anticipation had opened the gates of her senses; she was noticing more things around her than usual. The way the houses were perched on hills, as if they were sitting there looking back at her through eyes that were windows; trees, shadows, the way shadows of trees played upon the road. She opened the car window and the smell of cut hay and forest came rushing in. It was like Harry the real man had made the world more interesting and sweet somehow, added some texture to it just by being in it.

Everywhere she saw dogs. Straining on their leashes as they were walked, running up and down properties behind fences, sleeping on porches, like children on the laps of their parents. When she got to Harry's house she pulled into the yard. Juno came bounding out, followed by Harry. He was wearing a blue shirt that accentuated his blue earth-from-the-moon eyes.

"You're here!" Harry said.

"I'm here!" said Clarissa.

"Come on in. Want some coffee?"

"Sure."

She walked into his house behind him, thinking to herself: *I am in the house of a man named Harry, a man I do not know.*

On the walls were pictures of Harry and Juno, in various poses, everywhere. On mountaintops, on beaches, on a long beautiful dirt road. A few were placed in a semicircle atop a piano. It was clear this man was very into his dog. As was she. She noted they shared an important thing, this human-canine bond.

"Do you play?" she asked.

"Not really. Do you?"

"A little," said Clarissa. "I took lessons as a child."

"Someday you can play for me," Harry said.

The word "someday" never seemed so loaded, so puffed up with hope. To have a someday with a someone, that was a thing she had not considered likely for some time.

Juno and Zeus were sniffing each other up and a frenzy of intimate licking had started between them. It seemed raucous and a bit embarrassing, and that, along with the sudden presumption of a future sometime that involved her playing the piano for him, took Clarissa by surprise. Then Zeus did something she would have rather he hadn't: He jumped up on Harry and began vigorously humping his leg. Harry laughed.

"He does that sometimes with people he likes. I always say don't worry, he can't get you pregnant."

"Its okay," said Harry, "I completely understand the inclination."

Harry gave Clarissa the coffee and asked what she took in it.

"Black is fine," Clarissa said.

Then they walked out onto his back porch. Harry had a wide backyard with trees and plantings arching all around. There were many wind chimes hanging from the trees, and they orchestrated a gonging melody in the breeze. In the center of the yard was a pond in the shape of an infinity sign.

"Nice pond," she said.

"Yeah, I dug it out and built up the sides. It has koi in it."

She smiled. "Well, you are clearly a pond visionary."

He laughed. "I am very creative," he said.

They took a walk around the yard and he showed her sculptures he had made and placed around: a little metal frog under a bush, a ceramic owl on a tree branch, and numerous abstract metal things that crouched around, with moss and wood embedded in them.

"Big art," she said.

"Yes, it is art and it's alive, too, it is art that always grows and changes."

Harry asked if she was hungry. "I could make you a sandwich with bean sprouts I grow in my greenhouse," he offered.

"Ahh," she said, "a bean sprout visionary as well."

"I grow the best bean sprouts around," he said.

She wasn't hungry but she did want to see the greenhouse, so he took her around the side of the house where it sprang from a tumble of boulders, a bright-green box of life. Inside was a jungle of plants and vegetable plantings. Ripe heart-shaped strawberries. He plucked one and handed it to her. She put it in her mouth. It was sweet and juicy and the seeds seemed seedier than other strawberries.

"A strawberry visionary, too," she joked.

"My strawberries actually are a bit famous."

"I can see why!" she said.

"What do you want to do now?" Harry asked. He smiled and a circuitry of crow's-feet appeared around his eyes. He was not a young man, this Harry. Older than she originally thought. But he was not an old man, either. He was somewhere exactly between young and old. They were sitting on the porch again, with the wind chimes chiming and the sun glancing down on them.

"I just want to tell you that when I saw you the first day, walking Zeus, I said to myself, I want to meet this beautiful woman. You have such a beautiful face."

"Thanks," she said.

"You are blushing again."

"Yeah, I do that when I'm complimented by handsome strangers, or when I'm out in the sun too long," Clarissa said.

A few minutes later it was decided they would eat some bean sprout and cheese sandwiches. When they went inside they found Zeus and Juno curled up in a corner by Harry's wood stove, as if they had known each other for years.

"So cute," Clarissa said.

"So intimate, so soon," Harry said. They ate their sandwiches and then sat on his couch and kissed for a long time. While it started out tentative, it became passionate very fast.

"Mmmmm," said Harry.

An hour later Clarissa found herself in Harry's bedroom, which was beautiful and painted the most amazing gold with yellow overtones.

"I like to do textured painting," he said. "Can you tell what colors are on these walls?"

"Yellow and gold?"

"And purple and brown and a little red," he said.

Harry is adorable and he understands colors in a way I haven't ever considered before, Clarissa thought. When they made love, Harry said things like "Delicious you" and "That is nice" and "Yummy."

The next day, Clarissa could not stop thinking about Harry—not just what had happened, so fast and so sweet, but how real it all seemed. How could it be that she had just met this real man and suddenly been right with him, drunk coffee, eaten a strawberry, had a bean sprout sandwich, and then had sex? Was this what other people did sometimes? She decided to call her friend Molly.

"So," said Molly, "do tell."

"It is all so crazy."

"Go on, I like crazy. I can live through you vicariously. My life is nothing but e-mails."

"I went to his house, which he built himself, by the way, and saw the pond which he also built and ate the strawberries and bean sprouts which he grew and then we had sex."

"Oh no, you ate homegrown bean sprouts?" said Molly. "You bad, bad girl."

"And, I repeat, had sex."

"It is just like Persephone, in the underworld," Molly said.

"What do you mean?" Clarissa asked.

"Well, she was taken down to the underworld by Hades and ate some pomegranate seeds . . . and then she was, like, his prisoner for half of every year. You went to this Rasputin-bearded man's house and you ate his bean sprouts *and* his strawberries. Girl, I'd say you are in trouble."

Clarissa considered this comment for a moment. She knew it was a joke, but she did feel a little like she was in trouble. "I'm stunned by it all," she said. "It was just so fast."

"That is just what Persephone said. Too damn fast there, Hades! And you even had Zeus and Juno looking on."

"Thanks for this enlightening observation," Clarissa said.

The next day she received an e-mail from Harry.

"So I will just cut to the chase here," he wrote. "I want to see you again, when do I get to see you again?"

"What's your schedule?" she wrote back.

"You are the one with a job and a life," he said. "I'm just here all the time on my property."

Clarissa did have a job and a life. She worked inputting information for a local physician and taught yoga on the weekends.

"Well, I'm free after five most days, and on Sundays, after my yoga class."

A date was set. Clarissa would stop by and see Harry one afternoon after she was done teaching yoga.

During the week that followed, Clarissa felt that her life had shifted into a new and unusual gear. She felt as if she was inhabiting her body in a new way, more consciously, and she felt an awareness of every step, the way her hands did things like tuck back a stray hair. The automaticness of her seemed to be laid bare, and it was as if she was seeing that for the first time. Things she ate had richer and deeper flavors. Because of this she ate very little. Things she drank seemed extremely liquidy. The way they traveled down her throat reminded her of streams and rivers.

She found that she was ticking off the days in her head. The way she had felt before meeting Harry had been centered and calm; she had worked hard on that. She was a woman in the middle of her own imperfect but cozy universe, a life made of yoga stretches and yogurt smoothies, mornings with coffee on her back porch, taking in the day, evenings with certain television shows she religiously watched. She particularly liked her Wednesday-night lineup.

Now her days were filled with waiting. It was as if the real man Harry had shunted away her own real life with the possibilities of some other one, though she was not sure what it would be. She was a little annoyed, actually, by how fast and completely that had happened. She missed her old self a bit, the comfortable, un-anxious one, who was not *waiting* for something unknown to arrive.

The day did arrive, however, the Harry day, but Clarissa was feeling a bit worn out from the waiting. She had found herself quite sleepless the night before. Would she walk around Harry's property and eat his bean sprouts again? Would Zeus and Juno cuddle up so lovingly? Would they make love again?

She arrived at three o'clock in the afternoon but Harry was still in his pajamas. His hair was all messed up and she could see that he was not really ready for her to be there. He did say she could come right after yoga, didn't he?

He came to the door and opened it, but the smile she was expecting was not there; rather, he seemed a little annoyed, as though he had forgotten the invitation. As she went inside he seemed to shake it off a bit. Zeus leaped on Juno with joy, and again the two playfully licked and sniffed and romped about the room.

"Well, I guess they are happy to see each other again," Clarissa said.

"Have a seat, let me just jump in the shower, do you mind?"

"Not at all," said Clarissa, settling in on the couch she had begun to think of as *the couch of many sweet kisses*. As she looked around she noticed a lot of boxes were out and the place was a general mess.

"That's better," Harry said, emerging all shiny and steamy from the bathroom. He had thrown on some shorts and a tee shirt and looked sort of delicious to Clarissa at that moment and she was looking forward to at least a hug.

"Today was the right day, wasn't it?" she asked.

"Oh yes, today is the day, sorry! Want some coffee?"

"Sure," she said. "So . . . lotta boxes around."

"I'm in the middle of a big project," Harry said, settling in next to her on the couch. "So, whassup, you?" he asked. He let his lips graze the side of her face. "Want to go for a ride on my motorcycle?"

In the backyard, under a big black tarp, he unveiled a Harley. "Let's take her out! It is a perfect day for it." He handed her a helmet.

He got on and kick-started the bike and she heard the roar of the engine, which reminded her of a dragon in a movie she had once seen as a child. "Hop on?" he asked.

Clarissa swung her leg over the bike and then wrapped her arms around him. They pealed out of the yard onto the road and then began a long and dizzying ride up the side of a mountain. They swerved and negotiated curves and then hit a straightaway, where Clarissa thought Harry might have been driving way too fast, but she couldn't tell, really, as she had actually never been on a motorcycle before. Then Harry stopped and they got off the bike. "Follow me," he said, walking up a trail by the roadside. They walked up the trail to another trail until they reached a flat rock summit where there were two chairs.

They sat in the chairs and looked down on a huge view. Clarissa could see mountains, and lakes, and other mountains beyond the lakes. A whole world unfurled there, like a glorious rug. "Wow," she said.

"Yes, it is all mine, this mountain and that one and the one over there."

Then Harry told Clarissa all about how the mountains changed colors with the time of day, from a smoky mauve to a deep green to a charcoal. And how on certain summer days it all seemed cloaked in mist, like it was wrapped in a shawl. He told her about how he had seen a pileated woodpecker once there, so big it was like a peacock, or even a small mammal. "Have you ever seen one? A pileated woodpecker?"

"Can't say I have," said Clarissa. She felt complete awe at the 360-degree view from the top of Harry's tallest mountain.

After that they sat there saying nothing at all until Harry, this realer-than-real man, took her hand and pulled her toward him and they kissed. Then they just sat in the warm sun and a cooling breeze, which seemed to join forces to create the perfect temperature. After a while they hiked back down to the motorcycle and Harry took Clarissa to a bar along the highway where he said they made the best burgers in the world. And Clarissa had to agree, after just one bite, it *was* the best burger in the world. "Or at least it's in the top five hundred."

"You are funny," he said to her. "And so beautiful."

When they got back to his house the dogs were sleeping again, peacefully, and they tiptoed upstairs to his room so as not to disturb them the way some people do with their sleeping toddlers. After kissing for a few minutes they stripped off their clothes and made love again. By this time it was late and Clarissa had to get home, as she had an early-morning meeting at work.

"So . . . ?" It was Molly, texting her.

"So awesome, so otherworldly. So unreal really."

"A real man who is unreal," Molly wrote, "that is just funny."

"Except it is amazing," Clarissa wrote. "It is like I am an actor in someone else's life."

"Except it's yours."

"Right, it's mine."

"And the dogs even get along."

"It's like they're in love," Clarissa wrote.

"You have that in common," Molly pointed out.

"We are both dog people," Clarissa wrote.

"Love" is not a word that women of a certain age banter around easily. It is like the word itself has had some sort of curse placed on it ten relationships back. Utter it at your own risk. After Clarissa texted this text she felt superstitious, like something bad might come of it. She felt like the character Wang Lung the farmer in the book *The Good Earth*, which she had read in high school. When he saw that his son was beautiful and perfect and healthy he covered him in a blanket and ran through his town saying "Too bad we have a daughter, and she is pock-marked and sick," or something like that. In other words, you do not want the gods to see you too happy. She felt that way about even writing the word "love," even in the context of her dog. Like God might see it and take it all back.

"Watch out there, woman," Molly texted. "You are getting in pretty deep."

"I am," she wrote back.

A day went by and Clarissa was still feeling a humming in her bones from the encounters with Harry. She kept playing over the moments of him in her head. The cheek kiss on the couch, the silence on the mountaintop, the too-fast Harley ride to the mountain, and the bar with the hamburgers. She felt as if she had a video loop of it running all the time. And she was eager to know what would happen next with this real man, Harry.

Two days went by and she heard nothing from Harry. She kept thinking about him, though. His smell (which she had decided was something between clove and Drakkar Noir); his blue blue earth eyes, his cuddliness, his ability to take her completely by surprise with an amazing compliment. She checked her phone several times an hour for a text. She went online to see if she had an e-mail every twenty minutes or so. Since she had a job that involved sitting at a computer, this was really not that difficult. She actually kept two windows open on her screen. One was her work and the other her e-mail, just in case a message popped up. But nothing came along.

By day three she was getting antsy. Was he busy with that box project? She realized she had no idea what sort of box project it was, or even what he actually did with his days, beyond tending to his bean sprouts and strawberry plants and riding his Harley to the top of his mountain. She actually could not imagine a typical day in his life. The more she thought about it, the more she realized she actually knew nothing about him at all. About all the normal things you know about people, their work, and families and friends, she knew squat. She didn't even know his last name.

Day four arrived and Clarissa was getting frustrated. She had begun checking for texts and e-mails every few minutes. Finally she decided it was enough, and she texted him.

"Knock knock," she wrote.

Nothing.

"I just don't get it," she wrote to Molly. "What did I do wrong?"

"Babe, you might not have done anything wrong."

"But I just don't get it," Clarissa wrote again.

"You already said that."

"I know, I just don't get it."

"STOP!" wrote Molly. "You need to do something else, rent a movie."

Clarissa did just that. In fact, she rented three movies, and then she went to one in a movie theater and she talked on the phone to her sister, Eleanor. She told Eleanor all about the real man Harry and then asked, "What do you make of it?"

"Do you really want to know?" Eleanor asked.

"Yes!"

"Okay, you asked for it. I think that it was an incredibly foolish and dangerous thing to get involved in the first place. You went to the house of a complete stranger. You are lucky all he did was check out. Christ, Clarissa, he could have been a serial killer."

"But he's not."

"Lucky for you," she said.

After a week, Clarissa realized she was returning slowly to her "before Harry life," watching her old shows, starting out her day with her yoga stretches, doing her old favorite things. Making her protein shakes, looking out at the trees at the beginning of each day—but the enjoyment of it all was somehow diminished. Harry had shown her a different something, whatever it was. When she was with him she had felt the world was in bas-relief. Now all the textures seemed dull and flat.

She dialed his number but nobody answered. Against her own good judgment, she called again. She left a message: "Dude, I'm worried about you."

Finally she did something she knew could lead to great weirdness and possibly heartbreak. She decided to visit him, uninvited, or at least just drive by his place, the little house by the infinity-shaped pond and the property above, the mountaintop with the chairs. It was a rainy day, and the water sloshing over her windshield made everything blurry, like looking out at the world when you have been crying.

When she got to his house, she saw his truck was gone. There was no sign of him anywhere. She drove farther up to the mountain property but his truck wasn't there, either. Then she drove back to the little house and parked. She sat there a long, long time before getting out in the rain.

Immediately she noticed an odd nothingness in the damp air. It was the wind-chiming music that had rung from the back porch. The wind chimes were gone. The motorcycle under the tarp was gone. The greenhouse was there, still full of plants and steamy inside, but the door was wide open. She knocked on the door of the house.

Nothing.

On tiptoe she peered into a window. The whole house was empty! Everything was gone. The couch of many kisses. The stained-glass windows. The many odd sculptures in the trees that could grow and change. All of it, gone.

Juno, gone.

In her car Zeus barked and barked, as if he was terribly upset about it, too. Suddenly she realized with astonishment that one actually *could* tell if one's dog was lonely, something Harry had said to her about Juno when they first met.

Clarissa sat for a long time on Harry's porch, holding her stomach, which had a hollow and aching feeling in it, before it occurred to her. The property deal he was doing in town when she met him at the park, it must have been this. His home, his mountain range, his streams and valleys, that he had sold. The boxes must have been for moving.

The real man Harry, along with his entire life, had vanished.

She texted Molly on her iPhone: "OMG, real man Harry is gone! I mean it, everything he owns, his dog, his truck, his motorcycle, his COUCH even, they are just gone!" she wrote. "I am here at his house. It is so weird."

"Wow wow wow," wrote Molly back. "The couch even. Just like an online man!"

"I mean there is not one scrap of his stuff here, except the greenhouse," she wrote.

"That is nuts," Molly texted. "But then he did have that weird Rasputinish beard."

"I liked that beard," Clarissa texted.

A year and two months later she caught a glimpse of what looked like them: Harry and Juno. She was at a street festival in a neighboring town, with a strawberry theme. It *was* Harry and Juno! She was sure of it. Maybe his strawberries were in some sort of strawberry competition. Maybe he was there to collect a strawberry prize. She had Zeus on a leash and she quickly rounded a corner to see where he was going. It was *his truck*; they were headed for his truck.

"Harry!" she called out. Her voice rang out a little too loud and people were looking. The man turned. It *was* Harry. She rushed over toward where he was standing, across a street and a large parking lot, about to get in his truck. But Zeus, excited, pulled away faster, and his leash slipped out of her hands as he rushed forward into the traffic, toward Juno. Cars were honking and there was a near miss and she felt her stomach avalanche as he leapt forward, just missing a collision with a Miata by a hair. Then, to her complete surprise, once across the street and parking lot, Zeus lunged at Juno, growling, with his teeth bared. Juno leapt into the truck and Harry got in, too. They were leaving.

He turned once and looked back at her, with a desperate sort of expression, like a deer in the headlights of her, like he just wanted to get away. Then she heard the click of the truck door. It seemed louder than a door click should have been. In fact, he was much too far away for her to even hear such a sound. It was amplified, like everything around him had always been, realer than real. Harry started up his engine and he drove away, slowly, until his truck was just a blue smudge down the road.

Love Quiz

Think of this story as a quiz. The sort you complete at 3:00 a.m., when you are alone and online and have had one too many mango daiquiris with a friend named Amanda who told you at around 2:15 that despite the fact that you have traveled together to Thailand, Paris, and Israel over the years and it was she who was at your side when you had your abortion, she actually hates you. Yes, she *hates* you! She said it emphatically, sobbing a bit around the edges of her drink, which she was literally leaning on, leaning with all her weight so as to make an indentation in her bottom lip when she sat up to speak again.

"I do, I hate you, Ona!"

"Amanda, you are drunk," you replied. "This is the daiquiri talking."

"Then the daiquiri is a truth serum, because I hate you, Ona." She signaled to the bartender that she wanted another.

"Is that really a good idea?" you asked in a sotto voce meant to signal, *I really care about you.*

"Shut up, Ona. I hate you and I don't want advice from you. I don't want to even hear your stupid voice. You can go now. I hate you."

This, Amanda told you, is because you dated her boyfriend from college three years ago. The one who had been the love of her life, she confessed (three daiquiris and a Jell-O shot in), and you, if you were a decent friend, would have known that and would have never, ever dated Jim. But you did and that sealed the ultimate fate of the friendship. She sipped her fifth daiquiri and you collected your backpack. She turned away her face when you said goodbye, and slammed a palm on the bar. One last angry gesture.

Slam.

Door on friendship.

Shut.

Now you find yourself, in the wee hours of the morning, alone in your teensy apartment on West 10th Street (with one window that will not, absolutely not, shut all the way, hence the whistling wind sound all the time), trolling the Internet aimlessly, feeling friendless—as well as boyfriendless. Because you were dumped not only by Jim (the love of your so-called best friend's life), but also, in the three years since, by Richard, Marty, James, and Tate, the last of whom might have been the love of *your* life. The gestalt of this situation leads you right to the staircase, which leads down to the pit of despair, into which, by clicking and answering the quiz that pops up on the screen from an online dating site, you will now descend definitively.

But wait—this story will give you a choice. You can either go on to the next section (section A, the quiz section) or skip it (and proceed to section B) or skip both of those (by choosing section C).

Each section offers up a different scenario, a very different ending. *Which is how life is, right?* You make choices, like you did by dating your best friend's college beau, and you must take the consequences. Your life, in fact, is one big quiz show. Box or curtain? Door or package? Take the money or risk all to see what is behind door number 4?

But know this: As in the quiz, the choices in this story step up in risk. If you are a risk avoider, someone who can't handle anything unpleasant, it is highly suggested you do *not* choose the third option (section C).

(The author knows from her study of the research on risk taking that approximately 35 percent of readers will, at this very moment, skip forward to section C.) (Which is exactly what is wrong with literature today, the ADD reader, who just wants to cut to the chase, what they deem is the "good part." But that is a problem for another day.)

A. The Love Quiz

1. **What do you seek in another person?**
   a) **loyalty**
   b) **affection**
   c) **hot sex**

Well, loyalty is always good. You would go with loyalty, you think. But then what is life without affection?
Richard taught you that. He was loyal as the day is long,
but there was no warmth there. No afternoon smooch
on the forehead. No little hug at dawn, no sidelong longing glance in the supermarket aisle. So one must give
pause to the idea of loyalty.

And then there is the thorny issue of sex. As you
learned from Jim, hot sex can lead to a sense of great
affection, and affection can lead to loyalty. But not always, which is what you really learned from Tate. Some
people can be sexually stupendous, affectionate as all
get out, and then flip on you, just stab you in the back.
This is because they lack loyalty. So for you, tonight,
this night of daiquiris and breaking off of friendships,
loyalty trumps all. Hence, **a) loyalty** gets your vote.

2. **What do you think is the best route to a man's
   heart?**
   a) **his stomach (feed him)**

b) his mind (talk to him, relate to him, tell him all)
c) his penis

You definitely fed Jim. You made corn bread and those little Thai egg-rolly thingies—spring rolls, that's it. Plus you made chili and enchiladas and rice and beans and mango smoothies. You made Alfredo sauce so smooth and creamy it was like eating silk. You made those crunchy potato latkes with rosemary because you wanted him to enjoy some aspect of your culture and you were sensing a hint, just a smidgen, of anti-Semitism there. But then, two days later, when you were watching *Schindler's List*, he said, "Why can't the Jews get past the Holocaust? Isn't it about time?"

It was right about then that the tick in your heart, the uptick, that thing you had for him, with his mega paintings and darling *sol y agua* tattoo, his motorcycles, his bad-boy act, died for you. Poof. You shut your heart, and your kitchen, down.

So much for feeding love.

Now, you certainly understood the mind of Richard. You talked and talked until you were blue in the face. You discussed matters of importance. Issues of the day. You went to hear lectures by famous poets and politicians, like Netanyahu, even though you deeply disliked the man, because it is important to know what people think. Even the people you disagree with, right?

And Richard went, too, and then you argued, intellectually argued, over his ideas.

Once you argued so hard and so long it became dawn and you were still arguing (something about Kant) and you were in a coffee shop on 14th Street that never closed and the waitresses kept looking at you, like *begging you please* to pay up and leave, but you didn't, you stayed and talked some more and other people joined in at breakfast and they argued, too.

How funny was it when you all forgot what it was exactly you were arguing about, and who was on which side? It had all become a blur, a blur during which you noticed Richard had moved over to the other side of the booth and was sitting next to Liselle, glaring, in fact, at her cleavage. Liselle, who never had anything to say about anything! Liselle, who had just sat there with her steamy coffee, listening, with her cleavage.

Which leads you to **c) his penis**.

Now, Tate had a beautiful one. It was long and wide and had a sort of curve in it, like a relaxed banana. And, for the record, it matters. It may be terribly un-PC to say so, but everyone knows it. Everyone. You adored it and even worshipped it a bit, and he liked all that adoration and liking. He was proud of it. He even sent you a photograph of it once, taken with his cell phone. Which you actually kept. Kept!

But it turned out that one penis admirer was not enough for Tate. He was collecting admirers. You think now, looking back, he might have even had a Tate Penis Fan Club going. In the end, you realized you were just one of the card-carrying, or rather, cell-phone-photo-carrying, members.

So much for option **c**. The best way to a man's heart is not his penis.

So which choice, then? You pick **a**, because at least with Jim you had a nice time, eating and such. He might not really have been an anti-Semite. You might have overreacted. But then, dating Jim led to the loss of Amanda. Definitely problematic. Nevertheless, **a) his stomach** wins the day.

3. **You would rather:**
   a) **ski and smooch on the chairlift**
   b) **walk and hold hands**
   c) **swim and have sex**

Okay, this is a hard one. You love to ski. In fact, some of the nicest moments of your life were on ski slopes with the sound of the trees whispering, the distant *shush* sound of someone skiing down a nearby slope, and you, there in a wooded place, about to possess a sense of speed and even a personal ownership of gravity. Riding a chairlift with someone you will share this experience with, share while being yourself, choosing your own path down a mountain, is one of life's most romantic moments.

Especially when Marty popped out that little bottle of Drambuie and uncorked it and offered you his deerskin wine flask. Now, Marty was a mountain man with big hands and a knife in a leather belt loop holder at all times, ready and waiting for those manly knife duties such real men encounter. He was also a gentleman. You had so much fun at his A-frame cabin right on the slopes of Taos—well, not the actual ski area slopes, but the opposite side of the canyon, in a place where you could actually ski down to the first chair. That cabin had no heat, just a wood stove. It had no rooms; it wasn't even really finished being built—but the time you spent there was so wonderful, eating venison from the deer he shot, cooked on sticks (from trees he cut down) over the fire. Drinking more from his deerskin flask, listening to him play his mandolin. He suggested you might want to try eating some bear he had in his freezer at home. He was a bear-eating sort of man and he made you feel very cave-girlish. A *me man you woman* sort of thing.

Chairlift. Definitely kissing on a chairlift.

Everyone knows that swimming and sex don't really go together; it is sort of impossible to get the right position. It only works in movies, you are convinced of it. And holding hands on a walk—well, that is just something from Hallmark.

Now, tabulate your answers. Give yourself ten points for every **a** response, five points for every **b**, and one point for every **c**. You have earned the maximum, fifteen points! Which means that according to those polled by Loveforever.com, you are excellent relationship material.

Oh yes, there is every hope for you. You, my dear, will find love; the Love Quiz deems it so. On this note, you head to the medicine cabinet, take two Excedrin PMs, and go to bed. Life will turn around. Amanda will be in a much better mood when she sobers up tomorrow. It will all be okay.

B. Who You Are by Candlelight

Wait, this is ridiculous. An online "Love Quiz"? You are way, way above such drivel. You are too sophisticated. Too smart. Too educated. You have a master's degree in anthropology. Heck, you understand and know all about the research of Professor Louis Binford on the migration and trade patterns of the late Mayan, Aztec, and Olmec empires, which it is likely only one-millionth of mankind has ever even heard about.

You have better things to do with your life. You will do something better right now. Who cares if it is 3:00 a.m.? All that drama with Amanda has made you hungry. You will go to an all-night diner—not the one where you once spent hours arguing with Richard only to have him go home with a much quieter, less argumentative woman. Not the diner where your mother told you she was divorcing your father. Definitely not the diner where you broke your molar on a walnut shell in the salad during a job interview. You will go to the diner you love more than any other diner in the world, the Empire Diner, on the west side, where your friend Lizzie tends bar and takes orders for munchies at this time of night. You will go there because she is beautiful and sweet and always has an assortment of handsome men mooning over her, yet she still comes over to talk to you. Plus, she knows Amanda and might have some words of wisdom for you on this sad, sad night. She might offer consolation. She might, also, give you a free drink. A coffee and amaretto would be lovely right about now.

You walk in and there she is, Lizzie, in a halo of bright admirers. One has a tattoo on his neck of the Virgin Mary. One has a patch on his eye. A pirate! One has looked over at you—and did he? Yes he did. He just winked. He is blond and tall and has the nicest soul patch. You sit down and, before you know it, Lizzie has brought you a coffee and amaretto. The girl has read your mind.

At this late hour, the Empire Diner is partially lit by candlelight, and you have always looked your best in candlelight. There are four important zones of light on earth, you have determined. One is sunlight, which can be very harsh on the skin but grants most people a ruddy and healthy complexion after exposure (although skin cancer later on, alas). Two is starlight, which makes most every girl on earth look a little bit like a fairy queen. Or a ghost. Take your pick. Third is fluorescent light, which is the light of choice in most workplaces on earth and makes almost every human being except for Cindy Crawford look like death warmed over. Last comes candlelight. This is the kindest light there is. It makes you beautiful even if you are not and accentuates your beauty if you are. The most lovely thing one could ever see would have to be Cindy Crawford by candlelight. And you, well, you look pretty darn good in candlelight, too, which would explain why your three most romantic moments in life have occurred in restaurants with those little red glass candles on the tables.

Lizzie leans over the bar, neatly pulling her long braid away from the candle, avoiding every girl's worst nightmare—candle hair incineration—and whispers: "I heard all about it, hon. Jim slept with all of us, Ona. If Amanda makes that her criteria for friendship, she won't have a friend in New York."

"Oh, Lizzie, thank you," you say, *thank you*, you think, for the drink, the words, the caring, the involvement in your actual life, for calling you "hon." It is your philosophy of life that one must have someone to call one "hon" at four in the morning in every town one spends time in. To have such friends is priceless, golden. And now the blond winking man is moving over to sit next to you. He asks what you are drinking and then, before you can protest, he orders you another.

"So what," he asks, "is your favorite thing to do?"

You pause and look hard at him. Now is your chance to get something right in life. You must speak the truth, not tell him what you think he wants to hear.

"Where do you wish you were right now? This very second?" he continues.

"On a chairlift," you say, "with you."

"Really?"

"Yes, and then we could ski and go back to a little cabin, where I would make you the best pasta Alfredo you ever had. It would be like eating silk."

The man, named Stefan, smiles. "I would like to kiss you," he says.

"Be my guest," you say. In this manner you flirt and kiss until dawn.

You are assuming that your best friend will forgive you your trespasses and that, in addition, you have found new love, at least of a temporary nature, which can be satisfying, if not ultimately fulfilling, when one is twenty-nine years old and living in New York. You will take it.

C. You Survive, Sort Of

Because it is very late and you are still quite drunk and feeling very melancholy, you flip away from the love quiz to your favorite social networking page, where you see that both Jim and Tate are online and chatting. You flip a coin and it comes up Jim, of course. Jim is the male theme park of the evening, and you think there is some sort of serendipity going on. You must face it. You must confront it so you can move on.

"Hi-hey," you type, into the little rectangle. And push "send."

"Hey girl," Jim writes back. "Watcha doing?"

"Same as you, on here . . ."

"Well, I am doing more than that."

"Of course you are, so what, or WHO are you doing, if I may ask?"

"I am doing a huge doobie with Alex and John and wishing I was doing you. ☺"

"Really?"

"Sure, go grab a cab."

Your heart races. In fact it drag races. Your heart is going NASCAR on you.

Well, here is an opportunity to perk up the evening, you think. (But also neatly place a nail in the coffin of your friendship with Amanda.)

"So you coming or what?"

"Do you still live . . ."

Damn, you can't remember where Jim lives. Was it that walk-up on Rivington Street or the loft on Canal, or was it the huge building in Williamsburg? You must be really drunk; you can't remember.

"Yes, I do, right here in Red Hook. You know it well, Ona. This is where we . . .

"Oh I remember. ☺"

"I bet you do."

It is all coming back to you. Red Hook. Of course. Back when you lived in Carroll Gardens. Three years ago you practically lived in his place, full of his motorcycles and sculptures made of car parts. It was always a party at Jim's. That you remember best. He is sort of a walking party, more party than man. If he were a car, "Have party, will travel" would be his bumper sticker. And what sort of car would he be? A vintage pickup on its way to a party!

A 1959 Chevrolet Apache, turquoise blue, to be specific, a little beat-up but oh-so-retro-cool. That is Jim; you remember him well suddenly, in a sort of soft-focus way.

If you were a car, you would be a Ford Falcon, 1963, also turquoise blue. You would have the original seats and fuzzy dice hanging from the mirror. You would also be retro cool. That was what Jim saw in you, you think. The fuzzy dice Ford Falcon–ness of you.

But right now you are a girl who has had too many daiquiris being invited over by an old flame. *What the hey,* you think, and you throw on your purple boa and your motorcycle jacket and go out your door to catch what is likely the last cab in Manhattan on your street, which happens to be an old-fashioned one, fat and comfy with wide faux leather seats, and an Indian driver who smiles to show he has no front teeth.

You are in a movie. The movie of you, and this is the scene where the sun is close to rising and you are crossing the Brooklyn Bridge and it looks like a diamond necklace, strung as it is with headlights. You are twenty-nine years old and your best friend hates you because of a man you will soon see again. But is it a movie you would actually go and see? That is the question.

The cab pulls up at Jim's Red Hook studio and you can hear the party inside. Turns out it is a party of five. Five guys, and they are drinking Corona from bottles and a lime is on the table cut into nice little slices. They have put on a Nick Cave CD, of course, and there is some kind of movie on a large television. It looks a bit like a porno something, but you choose not to look at it. "Hey, babe," Jim says, sounding just like three-years-ago Jim, but something is different. He is gaunt and his hair has receded and he seems to be missing a significant front tooth. One of his incisors. It gives him a bad look, a down-on-his-luck look. Which reminds you suddenly of your brother Archie, who is a meth head in rural Pennsylvania. Jim's eyes look all flashy and weird, like Archie's do. "Oh God, Jim, you aren't? . . ."

"Drunk? Oh, I am. You are, too."

He sidles over and wraps his arms around you, so Jim-like, like coming home to somewhere you have been away from so long. And you wrap back but all you feel is bones. It is Jim pared down to the essence of Jim. It smells like Jim. It talks like Jim but it feels like less than Jim. Then it occurs to you; it is what is left of Jim, after three years of meth.

He has that methy thing going on and so do all his buds. They light up something that looks like a pipe and you realize then it isn't meth, it's crack. This isn't meth-head Jim, this is crackhead Jim. Or maybe garbage-head Jim. At any rate, it isn't much of Jim.

Then you see, too, the way his friends are looking at you. It is unsettling. They are looking at you like something they will shortly have for dinner. It is a hungry stare, a Hansel-in-the-witch's-cage stare. Suddenly you recall that comment, about Jews needing to get over the Holocaust, and your heart does a little backflip.

It becomes clear to you, in that instant, that you are deep in the bowels of an industrial building in Red Hook with five guys on crack. And right about then you think, *Okay, I am ready to wake up now, One two three, WAKE UP TIME,* but you do not wake up because you are already awake. And one of Jim's friends has his hands on your pants and the other has his hands on your shirt and Jim, himself, he of the Amanda-friendship-ending argument, is now pulling down your sweater and someone else you are not sure who puts his hand so tight over your mouth.

You are cooked, girl. You walked right into this one. The room smells of ammonia and vomit, beer and cigarette smoke, and one of the guys seems to be unbuckling. A pit bull walks into the room from the kitchen and bares his teeth; someone throws him a burger wrapper. His eyes are yellow. Get ready for your biggest nightmare, girl. Get ready to pray they let you up for air.

Let you live.

This is not the end of the story you might like, but it is the way things happened. The author has kindly spared you the most unpleasant details out of a sense of propriety and good manners. She has also provided two infinitely more pleasant alternative endings for you, in case you can't handle this one.

The author, who survived this experience and has gone on to become a reasonably stable mother of two in Westchester, understands if you are not comfortable reading this particular chapter of her life. The author understands that this might not be what you thought you were heading for in a story so innocently titled.

The author apologizes.

The Hypothetical Girl

For some time now Emily has been vanishing.

It began with her edges. The outside ones; arms, legs, back, and so forth. They began to go all soft focus, as seen through unadjusted binoculars. Next to go were her feet. She would look down and half the time they were hardly there. Ghost feet. Then it was her eyes. They looked like sketches of eyes. *Oh dear,* she thought. *And they were such nice eyes. Everyone had said so.*

She was like those islands in the South Pacific that are covered entirely by the ocean at high tide. Or those stars that are sucked up on certain nights by shreds of cloud. Here and then gone. It was troubling to see whole pieces of herself blur.

"I guess some people die and some people just disappear," she said to her therapist, June. She was seeing her twice a week now. "There is really not much you can do about it."

Some days she felt just like her old self. Very there. But other days she was not much there at all. She could walk through a mall or crowded street and nobody so much as looked at her. She could say hello or nod to people and they didn't even glance in her direction. *I am almost gone now*, she thought.

Naturally, you want to know how such a thing happens to someone. You are concerned that this could be something that could happen to you, and you would like to avoid such a fate. Was it something she ate? Drank? A peculiar bout of influenza or something contracted abroad, perhaps, when she went on that little tour of Micronesia with her friend Allison?

Could it have been the entire case of chicken-flavor ramen noodle soup she consumed last winter, after she broke up with Dane? God knows what they put in that stuff. She hadn't left her apartment for weeks, subsisting on ramen noodle soup and nothing else. She did not answer her phone or e-mails or check her Facebook page. She just lay in bed, feeling her limbs sink down into the blankets like quicksand, and read the entire oeuvre of Henry James. Then she read most of Flaubert and a good deal too much Maupassant. She read in the dark, by the light of a small flashlight. Reading and sinking. Sinking and reading. She gobbled books like someone eating chocolate. Guiltily, naughtily. To the exclusion of all else.

Philosophical query: If a girl reads in a forest and nobody is there, is she really reading? Is she really there? Is there any point to such a girl?

"Mom?" she shouted, into her mother's answering machine. "It's me, Emily."

No answer, despite the shouting.

She was trying to make a date to ask if she could store some things in her mother's attic, as a precaution, in case she vanished entirely. But how can you make a date if you can't even get someone on the phone? You can't.

To be invisible is a special status, and not an altogether bad one, she decided. You can watch other people in a different way. You can stare at them. It isn't rude if they can't see you back. You can be a kind of very personal anthropologist. She watched a man in Central Park feed his girlfriend a cinnamon bun in the most sensual way, section by section, letting her tongue lick his fingers at the end of each bite. She was tasting him and the pastry. He was like a spice. She watched a nanny whack a well-dressed child over the head with a newspaper, hard, to punish him for taking off his coat. "You will catch pneumonia!" *Whack whack.*

This is why they have nannycams, Emily thought.

For a time she wrote about her vanishing on her blog, "Emily's World": "I am disappearing. It doesn't hurt. It actually has no sensation at all."

Her therapist was quite delusional. She insisted Emily was still totally visible, that this was some sort of psychotic episode she was having. "Why do you keep referring to yourself as the disappeared girl? This is very unhelpful to our progress here."

"I am a realist," Emily said. "I call 'em as I see 'em. Or as I don't see 'em, apropros of the present scenario."

"Could this be a reaction to the divorce proceedings?" June asked. "To the way Evan took all the money, your nicest things, wedding presents and such, sold them on eBay?"

"I could have stopped him."

"But perhaps the way he treated you, so shabbily."

"It wasn't that bad," Emily said.

"Well, maybe it's a reaction to that man you met online," June suggested.

"Which one?"

"The one who said you were . . ."

"Hypothetical?"

"Yes, that one. What was his name?"

"Nick."

"Well, that upset you, didn't it?"

She had been mostly confused by Nick. She had met him on Matchmaker.com and they had chatted about six times so sweetly, so intently, before the phone call. "I think I miss you," she had dared to say, when they finally spoke with actual voices. "Can one miss someone one has never met?"

"You can, but it is ridiculous," Nick had replied. The next time she heard from him—and the last time—was when he texted her that sentence, the one to which her therapist June referred: "You are not an actual girl," he wrote. "You are hypothetical."

Yes, June may have hit the nail on the head. It was like a curse; he must have brought it on.

At the Bronx Zoo, Emily liked to go to the enclosure of the nocturnal animals, the "House of Darkness." She liked to see how the lemurs could blend so artfully into the leaves of trees; the bats could fold themselves up like unneeded umbrellas hung deep in the bowels of a closet. Certain toads could slink down into the stones beside pools of water and become stones. It was interesting to see the way these creatures vanished. They made it very artful. They made it quite lovely.

Her own vanishing continued to be a stop-and-start thing. It did not involve folding up or blending into trees or dark. She was more like a drawing that was being erased.

"I shall miss you," she said to the little bit of herself she could still see in the mirror in the morning. "You were nice to be. I especially enjoyed the way you looked in that red turtleneck from Saks."

Since she had lost her job some months before, she wasn't missed at work. She wasn't missed by a child, as she had no child. Her mother, in the beginning of her eighth relationship, which would soon morph into her eighth marriage (she was certain), seemed to be on some sort of extended pre-marriage, pre-honeymoon vacation.

Her ex was completely incommunicado. He did not answer texts, e-mails, or phone calls. His inbox was always full. She had the sense they had communicated for the last time when he told her about his new girlfriend. She had forbidden him from seeing Emily, texting or speaking with her. Her sister, Sofia, was mad at her for some long-forgotten incident having something to do with an Albuquerque City Bond they jointly inherited from their father. True, Emily had misplaced it. But she was sure it would turn up someday. Of course, if she vanished before it did that could be a problem. For this reason she dared not contact Sofia. Calling her would be like purposefully dialing up an argument.

Then she had somehow lost her cell phone. Everyone's numbers had been inside it. She could have tried to find them all, sent out some sort of frenetic e-mail to everyone she knew—*Send numbers! Quick!*—but it hardly seemed necessary if she was vanishing.

All of this had happened in winter, and by spring, when the first flowers tested the air with their bright fingertips, purple and clementine and ruby red, she was just a slip of a thing. Like cellophane.

She went out on her porch and sat on a small stool left there by the previous tenant. She looked all around at the ways things were coming into themselves. Then she felt something on her ankle. When she looked down she saw an ant crawling up to her calf. "Little ant, you are lost," she said. She flicked it back to the known world.

For a time after that she became water. She was a pond, a stream, the gathered drops in the tub after a shower. It felt nice to be so cool and shiny. Then she became shadow. That had been nice also, to feel sewn to a heel, connected. But then she disconnected and came loose and dried up.

She had known the day would come. She walked by a store window and there it was, the absence of her presence. In the place where she should be were other people's reflections: cars, women with strollers, couples holding hands, couples arguing, a mother and her daughter, two women who had to be sisters, admiring a lovely handbag. People not so different from the person she had been.

A man with a dog on a leash passed right through her and she reached out to pet it, right along its golden retriever–ish spine. For the longest time the dogs had sensed her, but this dog did not sniff or turn or register her at all.

She walked home quickly, feverishly, trying hard not to panic. She walked her invisible self up the stairs to her apartment and let her invisible self inside. The phone was ringing, but how can a vanished person answer a telephone? The only thing to do, the only responsible, sane, and viable option she could think of was to go to bed. Get into her bed and try to dream, dream of *being* and of things that are, of cotton candy and large spiral seashells, of brown spicy mustard and sketching her initials in cement when they poured the new patio at her parents' house; dream of the time she broke her arm falling off the jungle gym.

Dream dream dream of pain, of objects, of cold, of heat, of Jell-O, of potato latkes, of really really nice shoes. Dream herself back to the world.

She swiftly brushed her invisible teeth. She tucked her invisible self into her bed. She shut her invisible eyes and tried hard to smell the soft and slightly lemony smell that had been the smell of herself. She tried to feel her toes against the clean sheets. She tried not to be recently departed. She shut her invisible eyes and looked into the invisible dark.

Somewhere in the distance she caught a glimpse of the girl she had been before she vanished and she thought she would like to send that girl a note, letter, an e-mail, or better, a telegraph:

Dear me. Stop. You were real.
Stop. You had a few laughs. Stop.
It isn't your fault.
Stop.

Stupid Humans

Polar bear and deer were chatting. They had met on thosestupidhumans.com, which was not meant to be a dating site, per se, but then there were lots of stories cropping up about matches made there. Odd couplings, unconventional matches. Like eagle and sea bass. Now there was an original love story.

It had begun in a chat room about climate change, a concern all around these days, but then everyone else had left, one by one, shrimp, black squirrel, and finally millipede, and the two found themselves chatting solo. Suddenly it felt quite intimate, and deer had confided.

"Forest seems smaller all the time. They are felling trees like nobody's business."

"Tell me about it," polar bear replied, "you can't find an iceberg these days worth its salt."

"Oh, are they salty? I always imagined them saltless, chipping off as they do, from glaciers."

"Figure of speech, my dear," polar bear replied.

"Say, you ever get any terns anymore?" asked deer. "I hear they are in short supply."

"Oh, yes, we get terns aplenty, but they are just so annoying. Yap yapping, dipping into the krill and fish population. The whales are all so upset about it. They are turning into major competitors."

"Sounds like the woodpeckers. They are all over the place, eating all the bark."

"There you go, everyone is eating everything now, not enough to go around for anyone. Stupid humans."

"Stupid humans," deer typed.

Suddenly, there was an awkward lull in the conversation, broken when deer wrote, quite out of the blue:

"What is it like, the mating season? Any different these days?"

Another lull, then:

"No, there are females around, just can't seem to find anyone I connect with lately."

"I hear you," wrote deer.

"Now you, on the other hand, you I can really connect with," polar bear typed.

A lull. What to write?

"I feel the very same way," wrote deer, finally.

That was how it started. This conversation was followed by an exchange of e-mail addresses, texting, a bit of Twitter, and then a rather long ooVoo session when deer found herself quite attracted to polar bear, her heart all fluttery. Polar bear was also feeling quite out of the ordinary, all sweaty-pawed and a little, well, turned on, to be frank. Deer had such a soft tawny coat. Deer had such big, shiny eyes, rather like icy pools of water. And she batted those lashes so seductively, like pine branches in the wind.

They chatted all hours, ooVooed and Skyped, and the texting had gotten quite out of hand. Polar bear preferred to write at night, by the light of the moon. The days were so bright it was hard to see the screen. And with the northern lights flickering all around, well, it was just so romantic.

The problem with texting, as anyone will tell you, is the absence of tone. You just can't tell so much of the time whether someone is joking or serious, coy or aloof, sardonic or straight. On several occasions, deer assumed polar bear was rushing, trying to get the texting session over with. Polar bear had been doing nothing of the sort. But there it is: tone.

One day, very early, just after she roused herself from sleep, shaking all the loose chips of dream off her coat, deer shot a courageous text.

"Thinking 'bout you," she wrote. Indeed, she had just had a very sultry, sexy dream about polar bear.

Polar bear, at that moment, was already well on his way to sleep. He was so sleepy, just on the edge of a major sexy dream himself, and could barely rouse himself to respond. Polar bears sleep hard, hard, hard, and they love their dreams. He left the text unanswered.

"Are you mad at me?" deer texted the next day.

"What? Of course not. That is silly," wrote polar bear. "Why would I be mad at you?"

"Oh, I don't know," deer texted back. She was embarrassed to write that she was hurt when he had not answered such a personal and confessional text.

There was a lot of interspecies miscommunication, as well, having to do with feeding habits and migration patterns and such. Plus, obviously, the time zone disconnect. When it was midnight in the Arctic it was late afternoon for deer in her forest, so you can imagine how cumbersome that could get. Polar bear suggested they do away with texts entirely and stick with Skyping.

"I like it so much better when I can actually see you," polar bear wrote.

Deer felt her heart do a back flip. She blushed. When a deer blushes it is as if her whole body is trembling and trilling; it is very pleasurable.

"Awww," she wrote. "I like to see you, too. You are so handsome."

"Now it is my turn," polar bear wrote, "to say awww." Polar bear was blushing. When polar bears blush, a deep and warm flush of blood ripples through them, starting at their toes and moving up to the tips of their noses. Of course, neither one could detect the other blushing, as this was a text communication, but they just felt they somehow *knew*. They were becoming quite good at detecting mood in each other, reading between the lines.

Then came the silence. It was a rather long silence, caused when polar bear was forced to move to an entirely new feeding zone, quite a significant distance away. The fish were very sparse and there had been no sea ice to sun on at all in the area where he had been residing. But deer took the silence quite personally. What had she done, she wondered, to alienate him so?

"Hello, hello?" she wrote in an e-mail. They had not used e-mail much, and she thought it might get his attention. But polar bear used his e-mail only for very important business matters and communicating with a certain distant cousin in Alaska, so he hadn't opened it for weeks. He was having quite a hard time just existing, to be honest, and didn't want to trouble deer with all his woes; it felt like it would be whiny and very unmanly.

Deer, for her part, was feeling quite uneasy all day long. She walked through the forest despondently, barely stopping to graze or nap. Polar bear, polar bear, what happened here? she thought. Then, having lost so much sleep, she found herself falling behind her herd, and by the time she caught up all the good grass and twigs and such were already gone. She became rather spindly, and this was furthering the sense of a malaise besetting her. She tried to talk about it with a few friends and relatives.

"I am in love, hopelessly, I am afraid, and the object of my affection has just checked out. I haven't heard from him in almost a week."

"Oh males," said her cousin. "They do that. They will use silence quite strategically, when it suits them."

A strategic use of silence was something that had never occurred to deer. She assumed polar bear was straight with her, no game playing. They had even discussed it. Their mutual distaste for games.

Then deer did something she didn't like doing. She went on a popular dating site and looked for polar bear. To see if he had joined up and what his profile was. She found him. There he was: polar bear! He wrote all about himself and what he was seeking in a mate.

"I seek a partner who has similar interests, who loves the sun and warm days but finds solace in the snow as well. And . . . no games!"

Deer immediately compared her own qualities with polar bear's needs in a mate. She loved sun and warm days. She also thought she found solace in the snow. The forest filled with drifts and embankments, with sharp, taut edges. The world so thoroughly transformed. But then, was that admiration or solace? What exactly is solace? And how many girls had responded to polar bear's posting? She could see he had been on the dating site within the last twenty-four hours. He had gone onto the site but was not responding to her texts! This could mean only one thing, she thought. He was still "looking around"; she was not the solitary object of his affection.

Deer fell even further into her depression. She was thinking about polar bear all the time, she realized, and it was really affecting her ability to feed, move around the forest, and keep up. She became even thinner and weaker—not good. Not good at all. But from the point of view of one young buck in her herd, she was looking very svelte. He was developing quite a crush on her, and even feeling protective. He reached out.

"Little friend," he said one afternoon, "come over here, there is some very fresh sod to be had."

Deer ambled over and partook, hardly looking at the buck. Which made her all the more enticing, of course.

"Honey, what's the matter?" the buck asked. "You look so frail and weak."

"Oh, nothing," she replied, but she did notice the way he was looking at her. She could tell he was interested. If polar bear was dating around, she thought, she might as well engage in a bit of light flirtation as well.

She batted those long lashes that polar bear had found so delightful.

"Thanks for caring," she said.

"Oh, I care a lot," the buck said. "I really care about you."

Deer liked the attention but had to notice she did not blush all over or feel trembly.

Now, what deer did not know was that polar bear had fallen on severely hard times. The sea ice had all but disappeared and there was no way to fish from the steep sides of glaciers; he was in danger of starving. The time when he had gone on the dating site was pure accident. He had simply hit a wrong key and up it popped. Some kind of online snafu. It is a little bit hard for polar bears to hit the right keys sometimes, with those big paws. The rest of the time he was completely engaged in pure survival. Several young polar bears in his cohort had actually drowned for the lack of sea ice to rest upon while feeding. It was a gigantic tragedy; everyone was very anxious and panicky. On one occasion when he noticed he had a text from deer, he realized he didn't even have the energy to type back a reply.

Survival trumps flirtation pretty much all the time in this world, and this has been the undoing of many a long-distance dalliance. But deer didn't know what polar bear was going through, and she took it quite personally, this sort of game in a relationship. Or did they even have a relationship? Deer wasn't sure; the word had never been uttered. She certainly wasn't going to bring it up. That was the male's job, she thought. She was not a feminist sort of deer. And what was the future, anyway, for such a love pairing? The odds were certainly against them in the long run. But then deer was a magical thinker; she truly believed love could conquer all sorts of barriers. Look at eagle and sea bass, ant and sparrow! Love could be had in all sorts of ways, in myriad conditions, with all sorts of beings.

Love was bigger than clan, region, or species. Bigger than weather, or tides, or the politics of herd and gender. She felt a deep and pure love for polar bear, a real connection. This she knew. It was chemistry. It was kismet. It had felt determined to her by large forces in the universe, the pull of stars, the trending of seasons, the shared experience of the wrap and tangle of rain, snow, sleet. She really loved polar bear.

But buck had the home court advantage. He sensed that something was up with deer and asked: "Are you involved with someone? I want to know, because I am feeling a lot of feelings for you, deer. And I just need to know what I am up against."

Deer felt pretty much nothing for buck, and found him quite unattractive, with his bulbous nose and big big teeth. "I am quite besotted with someone else, I am afraid, and it is making me anxious all the time," she said.

"Who is the guy," asked buck. "Do I know him? It's an online thing, isn't it?"

"Yes," said deer. "It is."

"I knew it," said buck.

That fall the forest grew cold very quickly and there was not enough food to go around, but buck made sure deer got her share of feeding in and could stay alive. In his own habitat, polar bear was no longer struggling. He was a hardy, large bear with plenty of fat to keep him going, which helped him survive through the lean spell and gave him the strength to cling to the sides of certain craggy glaciers until the sea ice returned. As soon as he had a chance, he wrote to deer.

"My dear, my dear deer," he typed, "how are you?"

Alas, by this time, deer had decided not to reply. Polar bear had let an entire season go by, probably smitten with some young female bear, or someone he met online. She was not going to play this game. He had used silence strategically, to feel powerful and in control. And she had turned her attention to buck, with a heavy heart. At least he didn't play games. These online things were too confusing, she thought. Crushing, really.

Then, when hunting season came around, deer, besotted with disappointment and still very weak, was shot in the leg and again in the side by the hunter. She stumbled once and then fell down in a ravine, her gut filling with blood. She was dying.

Cowardly in the end, buck ran frantically away. She couldn't blame him. It was survival instinct, she knew it, and she was glad anyway, because it gave her an opportunity to text polar bear one last time. "I am shot," she texted. "And I want to say I have missed you."

"Oh my God, my love, my love," he texted back.

"I am shot. I am dying," she wrote. "I love you."

"I love you, too," he texted, "I always have. It was a hard season, there was no ice around and many of us died out, too."

"Stupid humans," she texted.

"Stupid, stupid humans!" he texted back.

Then the forest rose up around deer in a green sigh, the trees bent over her and their branches waved to her in the breeze. And she saw the hunter approaching, a blur of color and a flash of light, from the sharp, serrated side of his knife.

ACKNOWLEDGMENTS

I offer thanks to my friend Ruth Lopez, for her availability to consume these stories fresh from the oven of my imagination, to my cousin Stuey Cohen, who had no problem telling me when they sucked, and to my best friends David Margolick and Julie Eisenberg, for their unwavering belief in me.

To the gifted Jenny Lyn Bader, who will always read a rough draft and offer a smidgen of wisdom and humor (or a literary credo, for that matter), I offer my eternal thanks.

I must also thank my daughter, Ava, a girl who is patient, loving, and many other good things.

Lastly, I thank Judith Gurewich and Sulay Hernandez, my publisher and editor. Your enthusiasm for these stories will be ever appreciated.

ABOUT THE AUTHOR

Elizabeth Cohen is an assistant professor of English at Plattsburgh State University in Plattsburgh, New York, where she lives with her daughter, Ava, their dog, Samo, and their many wonderful cats.